D0395020

THE FOREST OF STARS

Also by Heather Kassner
THE BONE GARDEN

THE FOREST OF STARS

HEATHER KASSNER

illustrations by Iz Ptica

Henry Holt and Company

NEW YORK

Henry Holt and Company, *Publishers since 1866*
Henry Holt® is a registered trademark of Macmillan Publishing Group, LLC

120 Broadway, New York, NY 10271 · mackids.com

Text copyright © 2020 by Heather Kassner.
Illustrations copyright © 2020 by Iz Ptica.

Library of Congress Control Number: 2019949486

ISBN 978-1-250-29700-6 (hardcover) / ISBN 978-1-250-29701-3 (ebook)

Our books may be purchased in bulk for promotional, educational, or business use.
Please contact your local bookseller or the Macmillan Corporate and
Premium Sales Department at (800) 221-7945 ext. 5442 or by email at
MacmillanSpecialMarkets@macmillan.com.

First edition, 2020 / Designed by Katie Klimowicz
Printed in the United States of America by LSC Communications,
Harrisonburg, Virginia

10 9 8 7 6 5 4 3 2 1

For the stars who brighten my life:
Cameron, Moonie, Bill, Pop

How I love you

1
THE NIGHT THIEVED

The midnight sky darkened, black as the love bugs eating away at her mother's heart. If Louisa listened closely, she could hear them chewing. Tiny bites that crackled and clicked, as if their teeth were very sharp. And in the quiet of the night, when the only other sounds were the groans of the old building settling and the lonely call of a lune lark, Louisa could not block out the persistent nibbling.

She should have been curled with her blankets beside the fireplace, asleep like her mother, but the stone hearth had gone cold, and there was no more wood to burn. So she sat by her mother's bedside, listening to the love bugs tick and tock like a clock winding down.

In her hand Louisa held a threaded needle. Careless of the mending in her lap, she stabbed the pad of her thumb through the length of fabric. She held back a yelp and sucked the pinprick wound. With only embers in the hearth, it was much too dark for sewing.

Shadows crowded the corners and settled under her mother's eyes and in the hollows of her cheeks. They changed the shape of her face, sharpening every bone.

Louisa looked away. Her eyes fell on the pile of mending her mother took in from the neighbors, a task that afforded their food and their kindling and their rent, except that it sat there ever unfinished. Whenever Louisa offered to help, her mother gently refused her, insisting she was neither too tired nor too ill.

Though she would have liked to pretend otherwise, Louisa knew better. She tried very hard to sneak in late-night mendings, but tonight the gloom pressed in, and she struggled to focus on anything other than her mother's shallow breaths and the shuffling in her chest.

Louisa scratched her elbow and rubbed her knee. Sometimes she couldn't quite convince herself that the love bugs weren't crawling over and beneath her skin, burrowing closer to her heart no matter how tightly she locked it against them.

She'd heard their gnawing and chewing all twelve years of her life, but tonight they ate faster, as if they raced for the very last bite. Soon there would be nothing left beating inside her mother's chest. All of her heart devoured.

Darkness pressed in through the window. It spilled on the floor like tar, so thick it blotted out everything in its path.

Louisa set aside the mending and rose from her seat, levitating ever so slightly. She crossed to the window on nimble feet that never quite touched the ground. Maybe the shadows held her aloft. Maybe it was the air. She didn't know the how or the why of it, only the feel of it. Like there were marshmallows under her soles.

Soot gathered in the corners of the window. She peered through the hazy glass at the spattering of factory lights still burning and the darkness that swallowed everything else. The night thieved even the stars and the moon. With a shiver, she swept closed the tattered curtains her mother always left parted.

A slow breath wheezed from her mother's mouth. "Keep them open."

Louisa's fingers tightened on the fabric. She drew the curtain to the side once again and then turned back to her mother. "But it's so dark outside."

"Not any darker than when you close your eyes. And yours should already be laced shut by your lashes." Her mother spoke softly as she angled herself against the headboard, not quite sitting upright, not quite lying down. The shadows tried to hide it, but a small smile bloomed on her face. "I'm disappointed I didn't wake to your snoring."

Louisa laughed, pleased by the teasing. Maybe her mother was feeling a bit better. "I don't snore."

"You'll never know for sure, will you?"

"I suppose not." Although she did not like to turn her back on the night, Louisa drifted to her mother's bedside. "I'll just have to believe you."

"Now there's my sweet girl." Her mother pulled her arm out from under the blanket and reached up, trailing her fingers through the ends of Louisa's long, black hair.

Louisa smoothed her nightgown and sat on the chair once again. It didn't matter that it wasn't padded or that the back was very hard and straight. Not one part of her body touched the wood; a thin layer of air cushioned her, just as it did when she walked across the room or slept before the fireplace.

"I'm sorry if I woke you," Louisa said, though she was sure she'd been very quiet. After all, her feet made no sound, as they never touched the floorboards.

"Oh, no, it wasn't you." Her mother placed a hand to her chest, right over her frail heart. "*They're* the ones keeping me awake. They're so restless tonight."

Something prickled at the base of Louisa's spine, as if a love bug tiptoed across it. She squirmed on the chair. "I can hear them."

Her mother attempted to smile again but could not hold up the corners of her mouth. "Not for much longer."

Louisa froze in place, her lips setting into a grim line. She twisted her fingers in her lap. "Please don't say that."

"You'll have to believe me in this too," her mother whispered.

"I don't want to," Louisa said stubbornly. Her thumb throbbed where she'd poked it.

"Come closer." Already, after only their brief exchange, her mother's voice sounded strained from use.

Louisa knelt just above the floor beside the bed. She took her mother's cold, white hand in both of her own. "Should I fetch Mrs. Morel to mix a healing tonic?" Louisa glanced at the ceiling, where, in the apartment above, their landlord slept.

Her mother shook her head. "There's nothing more she can do for me, Louisa."

"What can I do for you?" Louisa clasped her mother's fingers. She would bring her extra blankets or warm water with squeezed lemons. Something to comfort her mother until morning.

A sheen of sweat beaded her mother's forehead, and a shiver ran the length of her body. She smelled of autumn roses after their bloom, something faded and oversweet. "Just stay by my side."

"I'm here," Louisa said in a small voice. "Where else would I go?"

Her mother's eyes flicked toward the window. "Sometimes I wonder."

"That's silly." Louisa never left her mother for long, not if she could help it. She did not even attend school, taught at home by her mother instead. "I'm not going anywhere."

"You won't mean to, but one day the wind might carry you away. The sky is vast, and like the Spark Woods beyond Plum, something you might become lost in. I could not bear to lose you to the forest of stars." Her mother drew her eyes from the night as if it pained her and settled them heavy and searching on Louisa. "You must promise me you'll be careful."

Louisa slouched under the weight of her mother's words and those still unspoken. "You have no reason to worry about me." But in truth, anytime her mother mentioned the forest of stars, Louisa quaked with fear—that the wind might blow her so high she'd float past the sooty fog and be lost forever in the stars no one in Plum could even see.

Her mother's gaze once again returned to the window. In the silence that followed, the love bugs licked their mouths and chomped off chunks of her mother's heart. They had never been so loud. The sound of their feasting rang in Louisa's ears.

"Mother." Louisa's voice quavered.

"I have every reason to worry." Her mother touched her tongue to her cracked lips, as if she did not want to release the words she'd readied. But then they fell fast and rough, pushed out from the place deep inside that had always tended them. "I think of it every day. That you might be more like William than I imagined."

"My father?" Her mother hardly spoke of him. Louisa

knew it pained her too much, that the very thought of his name fractured her already-broken heart. Louisa leaned closer so her mother could whisper the rest.

"Yes, your father." Her throat moved with the effort of swallowing. "Just before you were born, he lost his grasp on the world."

Louisa's thoughts spun all around, too fast for her to catch.

"He floated out this very window, up and into the air." Her mother clutched Louisa's hand, holding her in place. "I reached for his coattails, but they slipped right through my fingers. He lifted higher and higher, touching the clouds and moving with them as the wind blew north."

"What happened to him?" Louisa asked. Although she knew something must have happened to her father long, long ago (after all, she had never once met him), she hadn't known this secret. And she hadn't realized she took after him, that he too was made of hollow bones and too much air.

Her mother's voice crackled like broken glass. "I never saw him again."

But that Louisa had already guessed. All this time, her mother had waited for him to return, watching the window as if he might fall from the sky and back into their lives. He was the only one who could have chased away the love bugs.

Louisa had tried and tried, but all the love she poured into her mother leaked through the fissures in her heart, never quite enough to fill it or seal it or make it whole.

"I'm afraid for you." Her mother's fingers trembled. "So promise me. Promise me you'll always be careful."

Louisa didn't like the urgency in her mother's voice, and she didn't want to make the promise. Not because she wouldn't be careful, but because it felt like a *last* promise.

And last words.

Louisa bowed her head. There was not enough time for all the things she wanted to say, only this final moment to put her mother at ease. She opened her mouth but found herself too choked up to utter even the smallest sound. A silent sob rattled through her.

"Shh." The gentle shushing and the pressure of her mother's hand soothed the raw edges inside Louisa.

She swallowed. "I promise."

"Oh, my sweet girl. How I love you." All the rest of what might have been said trailed off. Her mother's eyelids fluttered and then shut.

Silence descended upon the room. A horrible, clutching stillness. It swelled and swelled, like a held breath, but her mother did not exhale.

"Mother?" Louisa said, gripping her limp hand, afraid to let go.

The quiet stretched on, a stillness more terrible than

the gnawing of the love bugs, which had ceased all at once, in time with the final beat of her mother's lonely heart.

"Mother!" Louisa cried. "Please don't leave me."

But her mother was already gone.

Louisa could not stand the quiet, how it engulfed her. Her throat clogged with tears as she released her mother's hand. She clutched her own to her chest, eyes bleary as she looked at her mother's still form. Louisa's heart beat fast, but she would not let it break. The love bugs could squirm through the smallest sliver of space or the tiniest crack.

She would not let them eat her heart.

❧ 2 ❧
SOOT-PRINTS

Every day since her mother's last breath, the wind wailed. It churned the clouds overhead and the smog coughed up from the factory's smokestacks. Black flecks blew all around, and a layer of soot stained the ground like the darkest, dirtiest snow.

With her skirt fluttering around her knees, Louisa looked down the street. Not a single footprint marked the blanket of ash.

And she would make none of her own.

When they'd gone out, her mother had always placed her boots down so carefully, perfect soot-prints left in the grime. They'd made a game of it, her mother an arm's span ahead, face turned back with a smile, and Louisa hopping step to step after her—no one in Plum the wiser that Louisa's feet never touched the ground.

But her mother was no longer here to guide the way. Not through the sooty streets. Not in any part of Louisa's life.

Taking these steps without her mother felt impossible, but Louisa turned up the worn collar of her black coat and stalked forward. The wind ran beside her, stirring up ash and twisting and tangling her hair so it whipped around her head like strands of black lightning.

Had she really been there, her mother would have braided it for her. Louisa could have done it herself, of course, but even the small act of plaiting one strand over another brought a thick ache to her throat. She would have given anything to feel her mother's fingers in her hair, how gently she worked out a snarl.

How, when her hands were busy, she might let something slip about Louisa's father. Little bits that Louisa collected and held close—that his hair shone as black as a starless midnight sky, the same shade as Louisa's own, that he was a night owl and sketched by the light of the moon, that he had once worked for the theater as a stagehand—but never once had she mentioned how he floated on air.

It seemed something Louisa should have known much sooner. It was a terribly lonesome feeling to have, every story of her father filled with holes so she could not see the whole of him. Not even the few spare photographs her mother had taken could trap his image, as if he was about to drift out of the frame.

Louisa took what tales she could from those faded black-and-white pictures. In one, her father ran fast with a long-tailed kite, his face no more than a smudge. It was taken the day her parents had met. In another, he stood just above the ground with his back to the lens, plucking an apple from a tree. And her favorite: the one with her parents together, their figures so small she couldn't see either of their faces clearly—and Louisa a small bean in her mother's rounded belly. They posed before a wide-striped tent, the sky above them dark but for the stars. Their fingers linked, as if her mother hoped to keep her father grounded. Louisa had always wondered where the photographs were taken, none more than this last one that she was a part of too.

As she walked along, Louisa glanced up, casting sad eyes at the clouds. She wanted her mother beside her. She wanted to know her father. The first was impossible.

The second was only *nearly* impossible.

Tears brimmed her eyes, but she couldn't cry in case the love bugs were watching.

Not now. Not ever.

Louisa let the wind numb her. She straightened her back, taking deliberate steps as she neared the crowded streets of Plum Square, which were surrounded by black-shuttered buildings so tall and narrow hardly any sun reached between them. Here, someone would have to look very closely to notice how her feet hovered above the ground, but she heard the whisper of her mother, reminding her to be careful.

Sidestepping a group of boys her age, Louisa clutched her bag. They rushed for one of the stands along the square, knocking elbows as they went and shoving schoolbooks from one another's hands, vying to be the first in line for a sticky bun (which was sure to come with a sprinkling of ash as well) or some other sugary treat.

She continued on, past the stalls with sweet rolls and scones and candied apples that smelled so much like happiness her lips twitched.

Louisa scanned the crowd, searching for the one vendor who was so inconsistent in her attendance at the market that it would be a wonder if Louisa could find her. All around the square she went, until at last Louisa spied the young woman at the edge of the alley, perched on a stool, two wooden buckets of flowers at her feet.

Although the flowers sagged in the bucket, all the best picked over earlier in the day, their heavy heads and velvet petals were as beautiful as the woman who sold them. They shone brighter than anything else in Plum Square.

The woman smiled as Louisa approached, an expression that seemed more appraising than warm. "Pretty flowers for a pretty girl? For a heart-sworn friend? For your most loved and cherished mother?"

The words chimed like bells and came as fast as the wind, blowing into Louisa all at once.

"What do you favor? The sweetest, rubiest-red roses? The hardiest chrysanthemums? Carnations to match your snow-white cheeks or asters to match your eyes?"

Louisa shook her head, finding her voice at last. "My eyes aren't purple."

"Come closer, then." The woman adjusted her thick skirts, layered teal, plum, and gold, which were so long they fell past her toes and swept the ground. Dirt dusted the hem. "Let me better see."

Louisa crossed the distance between them. Her fingers curled around the strap of her bag.

The flower seller touched the wilted rose struck through her hair and plucked off a creped red petal the same shade as her lips. Rubbing it between index finger and thumb, she leaned forward. Louisa squirmed under her sharp inspection. "It seems I was mistaken. Your eyes are a troublesome swirl of black and blue. But I haven't any flowers with me to match sorrow."

Louisa looked at her toes. She had not masked her feelings as well as she'd thought. "The daisies, please."

She and her mother had picked wildflowers each summer (before the love bugs had consumed so much of her mother's heart), arranging them in a glass jar once used for jam. Her mother had never said so, but Louisa had always imagined her father (faceless though he was) with a fat bunch of daisies in his hands, offering them up to her mother because he knew she loved them best.

Louisa slipped her hand into the pocket of her coat and tightened her fingers around one of the coins tucked deep inside, hoping it would be enough, for she could not spare more.

The woman reached down and plucked the flowers from the bucket. The stems dripped water, but Louisa accepted them without complaint and handed over the coin while nodding goodbye. She'd gone no more than a few steps when the woman called after her.

"That's a neat trick you have there. It almost looks as if you are *floating*. Are you a street performer? An illusionist? A levitationist?"

Louisa stiffened, too aware of the odd shadow that fell beneath her feet. She turned her head ever so slowly. "I am none of those things. I'm just a girl." (Oh, how she wished that were true.)

Her heart pounded in her chest so loudly that she worried the love bugs could hear its call. She forced herself to meet the woman's eyes, pretending she had nothing to hide and nothing to fear. The vendor made no comment, and her silence was even worse than the questions—full of *knowing*. Louisa shrank back, looking away and scurrying off before her secret let itself loose.

But the vendor's too-observant gaze followed her.

3
THE INVITATION

The sky darkened another degree, sooty air and nightfall overlapping. Prodded by the wind, Louisa quickened her pace away from Plum Square and the curious flower vendor. She'd come so close to being found out, and her heart would not calm. She clutched the daisies. No one followed, but she didn't stop until she reached her destination.

A spike-tipped fence surrounded it. Although she knew she'd spent too much time in the square and had come too late, she rattled the iron gate.

It was locked, just as it always was come sundown.

Louisa had no key. Not to the gate, not even to her old apartment on the other side of town. Mrs. Morel, the only one who might have taken her in, had put her to the streets the morning after her mother's passing, plucking the key right from Louisa's trembling fist.

She shook the gate again. She could not be shut out here too.

"Please open," she whimpered, but there was no one around to hear her.

The wind gusted harder. It swirled and howled and lifted her as easily as it would a feather.

Another wave of panic pulsed through her.

Her arm shot out, searching for her mother's hand before she remembered it wasn't there. She grasped for something, *anything*, to keep her grounded. Her fingertips trailed along the cold metal bars of the fence and then grabbed hold. She curled her fingers, tugging herself closer.

She stared between the bars at the cemetery beyond.

A darker shade of dusk settled in the bone garden, as if the night were deeper and the hour later on the other side of the fence. It swept a shadowed cloak around the shoulders of the tombstones.

Louisa did not trust the wind, which bullied her higher and tore the fence from her grip. It carried her up. It could carry her away, just as it had her father, all the way to the forest of stars—and the dark patches of space between them. Her throat tightened, as if she'd already floated out of the atmosphere and had no more air to breathe. The fence passed beneath her toes, the crooked gravestones too. She would not even be able to say goodbye to her mother before she was swept away.

Then, quite unexpectedly, the wind weakened.

It did not immediately set her down but brought her to a lonely, disused corner of the graveyard with hardly enough space to lay a person to rest, so crowded was it with willows and roots pushed up from the earth.

With trembling hands, she grabbed for the drooping branches and drifted forward, drifted lower, her black boots just above the grass once again. The air stilled. But she knew at any moment it could return for her.

Looking down, Louisa let out a shaky breath. She stared at the fresh-turned earth and the plain stone marking it.

Simone LaRoche.

Mrs. Morel had offered this kindness at least, paying to lay her mother to rest when Louisa had scrounged up no more than a handful of coppers from the tin atop the cupboard. "Keep them," Mrs. Morel had said, though she'd eyed them as if they were owed to her.

Louisa touched the stone, thankful it would always remember her mother. She sent *love, love, love* from her heart to the heavens and then scattered the daisies on the grave. "For you, Mother."

Still she did not cry. The love bugs—some of which had crawled into her bag along with her change of clothes, a well-loved book, and her mother's traveling sewing kit—craved softer hearts than hers, ones not guarded so fiercely. They scattered.

Louisa was very much alone.

Quiet, lonely days passed.

Each night, Louisa slept in the cemetery, resting just above her mother's grave, and each morning, grief shook her awake.

Louisa brushed leaves from her hair as she rose and stretched, leaning into a patch of sunlight like a stray graveyard cat. It warmed her face and sank into her bones. She tried not to think about winter, when snow would blanket the ground and ice would crystalize the tree-tops, so cold she'd freeze like an icicle sometime in the night.

As much as she missed her mother, she was not ready to be buried beside her. But the sweet memories of her mother were further from her mind than her mother's last words, spilled out like a secret, how her father had floated out the window, never to return.

"Where is he?" Louisa whispered.

The only reply was the growling of her stomach, and she clutched her belly. She had but a single heel of bread left, and she'd spent almost all her coppers. Although she feared returning and being found out, she'd have to visit Plum Square. She tried to distract herself from thoughts of the flower vendor who may have discovered her long-held secret.

Louisa stood, unable to turn away from her mother's grave just yet. "I wish you hadn't left me, Mother. I miss you so much."

The air sighed, as if her mother's sorrow and regret lingered in that very spot. Louisa walked through it, slipping past the willow's branches that tangled her in a hug before releasing her once again.

She passed through the cemetery, as quiet in the morning as it was at night, and out the front gate, which the groundskeeper unlocked at dawn. Plum Square sat due east, but she took a long, roundabout way—eating the last of her bread as she went—down the cobbled streets instead of heading there directly, all the better to avoid seeing anyone (or having anyone see *her*).

Her path also ensured she passed neither the small brick schoolhouse and the yard filled with children tossing soot-balls at one another nor the even-smaller orphanage overrun with gloomy-faced boys and girls. The administrators would snatch a lone girl from the streets, and then there would be no hiding how strange she was.

When she reached the square, vendors had already set up their goods for the day, staking out the busiest corners. Louisa skirted past them, and like the pretty flower vendor, she tucked herself into a less trafficked area.

Louisa set her bag at her feet, hiding the space beneath them. She straightened her coat and smoothed the knots from her unruly hair, because no one liked a beggar, much less one too ragged and dirty.

To her left, a gray-faced woman hunched over a small cart, whittling a slim piece of wood. Curled shavings collected at her feet. On her right, a tall woman with a reed-thin neck arranged necklaces and rings, bracelets and charms, setting them to their best advantage on a length of royal blue cloth. She stood beneath an umbrella, keeping as much of the soot from her jewels as she could.

The jeweler twisted her skinny neck, looking sidelong at Louisa and clicking her tongue, as if she could shoo her away like she would a mouse.

Around them, the crowd ebbed and flowed. "Spare a coin?" Louisa said from time to time, hesitant to call attention to herself despite her hunger.

Most everybody strode past, pretending they didn't hear her, let alone see her. By midday, Louisa had nothing to show for her time, and if she was honest, she hadn't put forth her best effort.

She'd spent most of those hours watching for her father, lost all these years, but maybe, *maybe*, not gone.

He had to be somewhere, perhaps caught in the dreaded forest of stars. Like the moon, which disappeared come morning, her father might be orbiting the world, watching it rotate so he could orient himself.

North, her mother had said. But that was hardly specific.

Louisa looked over the heads of the townsfolk, over the slanted rooftops and the factory's smokestacks. The sky stretched on and on, glimpsing more of the world than Louisa ever had. Her simple life had been enough when her mother was in it, but nothing tethered her anymore. She could go anywhere.

"Miss," said the woodworker, her voice as rough as her hands.

Louisa tore her eyes from the sky. "Yes?"

"Pay some attention." The woman nodded down the street and then leaned over her work, thumb on the dull side of her knife as she carved into a piece of wood. "You got a bit of charity. Best be quick before someone else snaps it up." She eyed the swan-necked jeweler, who had stepped out from behind her cart.

Louisa's head swiveled, and her eyes focused on an overthrown coin bouncing down the street. She hadn't even seen who'd tossed it. "Thank you," Louisa said, grabbing her bag and chasing after the copper.

It rolled several feet, then spun into the leaf-clogged gutter. As she hurried forward, Louisa glimpsed a woman striding away through the crowd, her long hair swishing as much as her layered skirts of magenta, indigo, and persimmon.

Bending at the waist, Louisa scrambled through the crackling leaves, sweeping them this way and that. Something gleamed brighter than a copper. There, tilted against the grimy curb, a glittering square of paper flashed black and gold.

All but forgetting the coin, she lifted the card by its corner and read the few brief lines penned in great looping calligraphy.

The Carnival Beneath the Stars
Magic, Marvels & Mystiques
The Spark Woods
Admit One

Louisa stared at the ticket, standing to better angle it toward the sun. The golden stripes shimmered. The glossy black stripes shone.

An invitation.

For the first time since her mother's passing, Louisa felt something deep inside her tremble with anticipation instead of grief.

A tickle of possibility.

4
TRAVELING WITH THE WINDS

Glitter sparkled on Louisa's fingertips, and the smallest smile brightened her face. It was an outrageous thought, imagining she could leave Plum on her own and see the carnival, but the longer she stared at the black-and-gold ticket, the more fervently the idea danced in her head and wiggled through her body.

Louisa spun in a circle. The wind turned her again, faster. Her dangling toes stirred up the dust below.

Across the way, a woman coughed. Her eyes honed in on Louisa, narrowing sharply, and then growing wide. She tipped back her feathered hat. "What trickery," she gasped.

"Oh no," Louisa said, unable to stop her rotation. She drifted inches higher. A cloud of black ash rushed around her like a whirlwind. On the ground, soot fanned out, streaking like the points of a star—absent any footprints.

The woman pointed and shrieked.

The man tending the fruit cart swung his head around at the exclamation. He ground his teeth and spat in the dirt. "Demon child."

Louisa shrank from the snap of their voices and the weight of their gazes. The jeweler poked Louisa away with the tip of her umbrella, nudging her higher still. The carver frowned, neither harming nor helping her.

The fruit vendor lumbered forward, casting out his arm as if he meant to snag the hem of Louisa's coat and drag her to the proper authorities.

Louisa kicked away his stretching fingers and darted to the right. She couldn't let him catch her.

Curling his lip, the vendor lunged. Caught between them, the woman with the feathered hat squealed and flapped her hands, resembling a scrawny crow that had not yet learned to fly.

Louisa lifted her legs, leaping over his head. Or mostly. Her boot struck his shoulder. He grunted, snatching hold of her ankle and pulling her lower and lower. She squirmed and twisted, striking his fingertips with her other foot until his hand recoiled.

Before she could flee, an arm looped around her waist

from behind, dragging her nearly to the ground. Louisa tugged at the hand holding her in place. Golden rings circled each pale, spiny finger. The jeweler! With a swift backward thrust, Louisa jabbed her elbows into the woman's stomach, and slipped out of her grasp.

Closer to the ground once more, Louisa ran.

"Come back here, you little devil!" the fruit vendor shouted, but she only sped up.

She wedged her way between the carts and stalls and chattering crowds, squeezing through the places too small for him to fit. Her footfalls made no sound, but his boots thundered after her, as did his voice. "Stop!" he bellowed, causing his mustache to quiver.

No matter how the man hollered, no one stopped her. Instead, they jumped back, mouths hung open, watching the sweep of ash and her feet tearing through the air instead of stepping on the ground.

She flew by them all.

In her hand, the ticket shook. She'd fled with such haste, there had been no time to tuck it away. But the sight of it gave her courage.

The sound of wheezing came from behind. She chanced a look over her shoulder. The vendor lumbered closer, red-faced and glaring.

Louisa pushed herself harder. The man's heaving breaths burst from his throat.

And then she was free of the square. The footfalls behind her fell silent.

"Don't dare return!" a deep voice called at her back. "Or I'll . . ."

Louisa raced back to the cemetery, slowing only as she crossed through the gate, ever respectful of the black-clad mourners, the poor dead souls laid to rest, and the somber, shadowed tombstones. She followed the dirt path to the neglected corner of the graveyard where the willows watched over her mother. Under the branches, the light fell softly.

Louisa collapsed by the gravestone. Her fast breaths slowed, though her heart continued to pound.

Everyone in Plum Square had turned to her and stared, some with curiosity, others with fright. They'd thought her so strange. They'd thought she did not belong.

How careless she had been to let them see what she truly was.

Louisa brushed dried leaves from her mother's grave and looked at the spray of daisies with their wilted stems and curling white petals. A beetle crawled through the dirt.

"I don't know what to do," she said.

But the moment in the square, the man's mustache bristling as he yelled, had all but decided for her. It did Louisa no good staying here, where no one cared what became of her, where she hadn't a single friend or a place to call home. Her mother would not want her moping and glooming over her grave. She'd want Louisa to be brave.

"Look what I found." Louisa held out the ticket for the Carnival Beneath the Stars. The willow's long branches swayed, filtering beams of sunlight so the black-and-gold stripes seemed to spin like a carousel. "Isn't it beautiful?"

When the flushed winds of autumn blew in and the first leaves seeped red, the carnival made its home in the Spark Woods. Louisa had never been, but for years and years she'd listened to Mrs. Morel's children thrilling over its wonders. She could almost call it to life in her mind. Acrobats flying through the air in sparkling leotards, wings sprouting from their backs. Long-tailed horses prancing in a ring as their coats changed from black to gold. Contortionists bending into impossible shapes, somehow boneless, somehow *spine*less.

A place where someone like Louisa would not stand out so obviously.

"I always thought we'd go together," Louisa said. "Someday."

She ran her fingers along the shiny stripes of the invitation, wondering at their familiarity. Like a dream drifting out of reach, a whispering sensation passed through her, a feeling that she'd seen something like this before. But that couldn't be, for she had never once left Plum.

Around her, everything was still. Louisa pulled her

mother's favorite book from her bag, fingers gentle on the tattered cover as she cracked it open. She read the first line.

Not so very long ago, a girl smiled knowingly.

Her mother's voice echoed in her head, the way it lilted up no matter how tired she was, always heartfelt in her storytelling. Louisa tucked the ticket between the pages, holding the memories close.

She flipped a few pages forward, finding her treasured photographs. Immediately, her eyes caught on the image of her mother and father in front of a tent.

A *striped* tent, just like the stripes decorating the invitation.

She closed the book, clutching it to her chest. Holding it right over her heart. Her parents might have—they *must* have—gone to the carnival long ago, and now, Louisa could do the same. She'd felt so aimless, but she had an opportunity to visit the only place she knew of with a connection to them.

Far off, wind chimes tinkled. A tune both melancholy and magical whispered in the air.

Louisa tilted her head, listening to the silvery notes. They softened the words she spoke next. "I'm going to leave you for a while. It's no longer safe for me here." But that wasn't quite the whole of it. She would be chasing after the ghosts of her parents too. All the words on her tongue caught in her throat. "Goodbye," Louisa whispered at last.

Before tears could squeeze from her eyes, she clambered to her feet and marched through the cemetery. A lone mourner stared blankly at a granite headstone. Out of sight, love bugs skittered, honing in on the muggy scent of grief. Louisa hurried past.

At the gate, she glanced back, but only for a moment. Just long enough to blow a kiss for her mother.

That very night, she'd follow the road out of town and head north for the Spark Woods. She could not follow in her mother's sooty footsteps on this journey; instead, she would be traveling with the winds—just like her father.

⤙ 5 ⤚
THE CARNIVAL BENEATH THE STARS

Giant maples speared the sky, a gateway to the Spark Woods. Louisa tipped back her head and stared up at the trees. They hadn't looked so large from a distance, just a blur of autumn color hung like a painting, but standing beneath them, she felt very small. The world around her was so much wider than she had imagined.

She did not know what lay beyond the bend, but the tickle at the back of her neck reminded her it would be far better than what lay behind. Any of the vendors might have notified the proper authorities and sent them after her. She cast a nervous glance over her shoulder.

All was quiet and still. Yet she hurried ahead, not trusting that they'd leave her be.

The road swiftly transitioned from cobblestones to dirt as she crossed into the wilder lands. Shade trees canopied the way, a lacework of orange and red foliage. And the wind, as always, hastened her along.

It had a different feel here, unhindered by the smooshed-together buildings and the smog that had smothered her lungs in Plum. The breeze rushed by, free of confines and corners, bright with the scent of crisp leaves and sour apples overripe on their branches.

She plucked one down as she walked, and it reminded her of the photograph of her father doing the same. Though soft spots bruised the skin and its flesh was rather mealy, eating it quieted the grumbling in her belly and the loneliness in her heart. She felt an unusual closeness to her father. Maybe he really had passed through this way once.

And if so, had he hoped to reach the same destination? Her father might have been chased from Plum just as she was. If he belonged nowhere else, maybe he had settled at the carnival, dazzling crowds with an airborne performance alongside the other strange and wonderful feats.

A gust of wind shivered by, carrying back bubbles of laughter. Ahead, the shadowed outlines of two women and a young child wove in and out of view, following the curves in the road. Like Louisa, they could only be headed for the carnival. She trailed after them, as if she brought up the tail end of a parade, except no one stood to the side of the road waving and cheering. Only the maples witnessed her passage, branches swishing like scattered applause.

Louisa peered into the hooded greenery. The woodlands breathed, soft sighs and birdsong. And deeper, the forest echoed with sounds of the carnival. She stepped away from the road and into the woods, following the music. She liked to think her father had gone the same way.

Louisa unclasped the top button on her coat, walking faster and faster until she was running. Her bag thumped against her side. Still her boots never touched the ground. She chased all the hopes inside her and the sundown glow stealing across the treetops. It streaked golden ribbons through the sky and ignited the leaves.

The woods felt alive in a way the town of Plum did not. Or maybe it was Louisa who felt more alive here, able to expand her lungs without that sharp feeling pinching the back of her throat, clogged with unshed tears. She drew in a deep breath, skipping inches off the ground.

Bit by bit, the sky darkened.

Yet Louisa had no trouble finding her way. A hazy light rose above the treetops, and the pinpoint tip of a black-and-gold tent pitched past the shadowed branches. Louisa ran forward headlong, as if the carnival might disappear before she reached it.

The swelling notes of a fiddle and laughter and clapping, the scents of cotton candy and salty-sweet kettle corn, and the ringing of the wind chimes threading through it all tugged her closer and closer.

She passed a pond on her left. It shimmered, reflecting the last rays of the sunset. Two small boats bobbed at the dock, and a third skimmed the water, led on the thinnest of silver threads by black-and-gold butterflies with wingspans as large as Louisa's thumb-linked hands. It looked like something from a dream, brought to life!

Beyond the pond and the line of people waiting for a boat ride, the trees thinned. In a clearing surrounded by black-barked maples, the carnival glowed beneath the stars. Louisa stopped all at once. Her heart tumbled around in her chest, and her dark eyes went wide.

At least a dozen black-and-gold-striped tents sat here and there in the leaf-strewn field, the largest of all right at the center. In the spaces between sat all manner of attraction and gilded carts with matching awnings.

She edged closer, peeking at the fringes of the torch-lit carnival as she walked the perimeter. Every face she glimpsed tilted toward the sights, brightened by the spectacle, cheeks rosy from laughter and the brisk autumn air.

The fair enchanted her so completely that she didn't even notice the makeshift fence of barb-wrapped wood until she stumbled into it. It snagged on her coat, keeping her and anyone else who might have ventured off the road from slipping past.

But Louisa had an invitation, tucked carefully between

the pages of her mother's book, so she had no need to sneak.

She smiled, poking her hand into her bag and pulling out the storybook. It fell open to the very place the small card rested.

Another gust of wind swept by, fluttering the well-worn pages and snatching up the ticket before Louisa could catch it. She gasped.

Too late, she thrust her hand into the air. Her fingertips brushed the pointed corner of the ticket, then it blew over the fence with a misfit of fallen leaves.

"No," she said, a sound so soft the wind muffled it.

She bowed her head over the book. All that remained of the ticket was a sprinkling of golden glitter that shimmered in the moonlight.

The words on the page blurred before her eyes. She blinked them clear, slapping shut the book and shoving it into her bag.

Louisa set her jaw, contemplating the fence and the wire of barbs strung around it. There was no way to climb it, she was sure, not without suffering a hundred sharp cuts to her hands and tearing her tights to shreds.

But not so long ago (and not altogether purposely), she'd scaled the fence surrounding the graveyard—and it had stood much taller than the one before her. True, the wind had done most of the work, blustering about as it had, but perhaps it would help her again. She stood very still, waiting.

Only, the breeze seemed more intent on blowing her hair into her face than lifting her body over the fence. She shoved the wild strands behind her ears and sucked in a determined breath.

At once, she felt lighter. As hollow-boned as a bird.

All those times her mother had reminded her to exhale deeply and stay grounded ran through her head. The way she had always kept Louisa so very close.

Louisa released the ghost of her mother's hand.

She inhaled again and felt lighter still. The wind buffeted against her. Instead of resisting its pull, she leaned into the gust, letting it carry her.

Up, up, up she went, rising into the air and over the fence.

6

WALKING ON AIR

Louisa had not meant to drift so high. It was thrilling, having such abandon; it was terrifying, having so little control. She clutched her bag, not at all sure how to get down. The wind had yet to release her.

It tossed her about, drawing her away from the fence and closer and closer to the tents, and beyond them, to the crowds. She could not let anyone see her, but the more she worried about being discovered or floating away, the more her breath heaved in and out, and so she remained aloft. Her legs kicked uselessly at the air.

And then her boot struck something solid.

"Watch it," a voice grunted from below. She twisted, glancing down and over her shoulder. A dark-haired boy looked up at her, a pinched expression on his narrow, olive face. He rubbed his temple where her boot must have hit him. His eyes flashed gold in the moonlight. "That was quick."

She didn't know what he was talking about or how he'd sneaked up on her, but it hardly mattered. He'd spotted her hovering five feet off the ground, and there was nothing she could do to make him un-see her strange predicament. Twice over, she'd broken her promise to her mother to be careful.

Louisa's heart thudded fast.

The boy reached up with one hand, snatched her ankle, and tugged.

All at once, it felt like she weighed a thousand pounds. It was a strange sensation, a sudden heaviness in her limbs she'd never known before. She descended in a rush, knocking the boy to the ground.

Of course, she landed just above the browning grass and his sprawled body, so she recovered from the fall more quickly than he did. She righted herself, collected her bag, and, before he could stop her, darted away.

"Hey!" he hollered, an echo of the vendor's angry voice from Plum Square. "Get back here, you sneak! I'm not done with you!"

Louisa kept going, not trusting his intentions. At best, he would boot her from the carnival. At worst, he would insist the authorities drag her back to Plum for trespassing. Who knew what they would do with her then—toss her into a jail cell to rot (unlikely, she had to admit) or turn her over to the orphanage where she would spend the rest of her days in the kitchen, scrubbing burnt oatmeal from dirty old pots (more likely, but no better).

Although his sharp voice chased her, the sounds ahead rang louder. Louisa dashed between two of the smaller tents, leaping over the staked ropes that seemed to be placed there just to trip her, and into the heart of the carnival. She wove her way through the crowd until she could no longer hear the boy calling for her to stop.

Still wary, she slowed, trying to convince herself that she'd lost him as she surveyed the spectators. That he wouldn't find her.

Perhaps he hadn't gotten a good look at her face in the shadows and wouldn't recognize her among all the other children in attendance.

Except no one else wandered alone. Girls with fuzzy coat collars strolled arm in arm with their friends; lanky boys walked three astride, cackling at one another's jokes; and the younger children, wide-eyed and laughing, bounced along beside their parents.

The absence of Louisa's mother ached all the more.

Without getting *too* close, she tagged along behind a family overrun with kids, hoping it looked like she belonged with them. A sullen older sister who would rather have been there with her friends.

She peeked over her shoulder, scanning every face, relieved when there was no sign of the boy among them. Though maybe he crept closer without notice, moving along the shadowy corners, ready to pounce when she least expected him.

Mindful of her footsteps, Louisa swung back around and tried to calm herself. She raised her eyes to the sights, but they did little to settle her racing heart.

The carnival vibrated around her, a tingling sensation that danced all the way to her toes. It hummed with music, stringed instruments clashing in an oddly harmonious way with flutes and wind chimes. Gilded carts overflowed, some heaped with sparklers, beaded necklaces, and golden crowns, while others offered caramel apples, pumpkin ale, and plum pies small enough to carry in the palm of your hand.

She wished her mother could have seen it too.

But she had. Louisa was certain of it now. In awe, she looked up and up and up at the great tents before her, identical to the wide-striped tent in the photograph with her parents.

Louisa would have liked them beside her right then, but she wasn't lonesome. She'd caught the thread of them. Or at least the thread of her father. For the second time that day, Louisa felt she truly was following the same path he had.

She would not let go of the thread.

The carnival glinted with an air of magic, just like the lost ticket had promised. Overhead, flames glowed in glass orbs, as if someone had captured fallen stars and strung them, still burning and bright, across the walkway.

But for all the carnival dazzled, it also hummed with darkness. Long lines formed in front of the tents, people waiting until the appointed hour for the performances. The first wooden sign Louisa passed was decorated with artfully stroked slashes of black paint that read:

Merciless the Spider: Shadow Spinner

She shivered, no fonder of spiders than she was of love bugs. Especially one described as *merciless*. The promise of a shadowy act (if she was brave enough to enter the tent) sounded like the makings of a nightmare. She was glad when the family she trailed did not linger.

Again, Louisa glanced back, fearing the boy had caught sight of her and sneaked through the crowd, ready to clamp his hand around her wrist the way he'd grabbed her ankle. But if he was behind her, his angular face remained hidden within the crowd.

When Louisa turned back around, the family had stopped in the middle of the path, and she nearly collided with them. "Sorry," she mumbled, but they were too busy pointing here to there, trying to agree on which show to see first that they seemed not to notice her at all. One of the children, a golden crown overlarge on his head, darted away from the others. All the rest followed, taking their place at the end of a very long line. Louisa craned her neck to read the sign.

Mina the Mirror: Magician of Magnificence

This attraction seemed a much more sensible, and much less frightening, choice. But though she was tempted to join them, she walked on, telling herself she stood out no more than she had in Plum Square where everyone ignored her until that very day.

With keen eyes, Louisa searched for a particular kind of performance, one that showcased a very specific ability.

As she went along, she scanned each board.

Fire–Red Rosalyn: Igniter of the Spark Woods

Strong the Ox: Boy Beast

Lovely Valentine: The Living Tattoo

Only, none of the signs hinted at the trick of walking on air.

None of the signs led to her father.

7

THE WINGLESS RAVEN

Louisa strode forward. She had glimpsed only a small portion of the carnival. There was so much more to see, and she might find her father just ahead.

Or, maybe not *just* ahead, for a grouping of carts with flapping black-and-gold banners took up the space between the tents, and beyond them, another lively crowd formed.

Someone shrieked.

But above the cry of alarm came the sound of laughter. A child sprang into the air, arms splayed, and then she fell downward, out of sight behind the gilded carts and the *ooh*ing crowd. Louisa watched, breathless. In the next heartbeat, the girl rose again. Her hair whipped back from her face, exposing a smile so wide her teeth flashed.

Louisa skirted the carts, and the long line of children

awaiting their turn, and found herself in front of a sign that proclaimed:

THE SPIDER'S WEB
A MOST FRIGHTFUL DELIGHT!

Louisa lifted up to her tiptoes and peered over and between the people in front of her. A web, blacker than the night and impossibly large, stretched taut from the burnt and twisted trunks of three long-dead maple trees. Someone, *something*, had threaded it so carefully, so precisely, it mirrored the spiraling pattern a spider would weave.

And within it, a girl bounced wildly.

Louisa placed her hand to her mouth, covering its O of surprise. Awestruck, she stared. Instead of trapping the girl as a real spider's web might, its silky strands formed a trampoline beneath her. No wonder the children jostled and shoved, pressing closer and closer, wanting to be the next to have a go at it.

Louisa's eyes swung up and down. As the girl bounced higher still, she screeched, probably from a tangle of fear and exhilaration much the same as Louisa felt whenever she lifted into the air unexpectedly. And then the girl plummeted back toward the webbing. It caught her gently only to toss her skyward again.

On the descent, Louisa's gaze lingered on the crowd.

All eyes followed the girl's rise and fall, except for one golden pair, which locked tight on Louisa.

The boy had found her.

Her smile slipped away, and the boy grinned, as if he'd stolen the expression from her face and taken it for his own. Louisa froze.

Circling the web trampoline, he scrambled through the crowd. Small spaces seemed to open for him as he approached, or else his elbows were very sharp and very well aimed, nudging people out of the way. Louisa didn't know why he was so determined to stop her, but she couldn't let him. She gripped the strap of her bag, turned on her heel, and ran.

She might have worried about making a scene, but there were plenty of other children darting from tent to tent or chasing after their siblings, laughing uproariously. But she doubted any of them feared what would happen if caught.

Frantically, she looked all about, searching for a place where the boy would not immediately spy her. Ahead, she spotted one of the tents she'd passed earlier. Only now, the people in line moved forward, the very last of them trickling through the open flaps. She ducked in behind them, and the curtain fell closed at her back.

It took a moment for her eyes to adjust to the dim. Glass orbs glimmered with golden light, strung from the tent's wooden poles, but they were smaller, the flames softer than those burning outside. Even under the striped canvas, Louisa felt as if she stood beneath the stars. Only the sky was strangely shaped, with peaks and corners.

Four rows of benches ringed the tent, pressed around the small raised platform in the center. With silent, air-touched steps, Louisa slipped into the very last one and hunkered down on the bench. Out of habit, she placed her bag at her feet to block the space beneath them, while her long hair and the fall of her coat hid the narrow gap where she hovered just above the bench.

From the center of the tent, the fire lamps flared. A voice rang out. "Gents! Ladies! All other lovelies!" He pointed to the children in the crowd. "And of course, you little beasts and terrible brats too!"

Laughter rippled through the tent, and then the crowd, vibrating so loudly only moments before, lowered their voices. Without quite intending to, Louisa leaned forward, eyes trained on the broad-shouldered man who'd spoken. Her fingers twisted in the strap of her bag, wondering if he could possibly be her father.

But no, no, before she imagined every man her father, she looked down to his feet. They quite clearly touched the ground. As he paced, he kicked up leaves that had swept into the tent, and his boots left imprints in the dirt. Maybe he was a strongman, then, Louisa reasoned, for he was tall and heaped with muscles.

"I'm just a man," he said, and it almost seemed he spoke directly to Louisa, an apology of sorts that he couldn't be who she'd hoped for. "My name is Bubba Wild, but there's no reason you'll remember that once you leave here today. After all, it's just a name, and as I said, I'm just a man. Nothing more, nothing less. Nothing special." He commanded attention despite his humble words. His lip hitched. "But let me introduce you to someone you will remember, most fondly and forever. Let me introduce you to Lovely Valentine."

Louisa remembered that name from one of the placards. *The Living Tattoo.*

The man tore off his shirt, and there, on the bicep of his right arm, directly beneath the tattoo of a faded heart, was the inked figure of the most beautiful girl Louisa had ever seen. She had dark hair down to her waist and lips as red as blood.

Louisa stared, caught by the beauty of the tattoo, but moments later disappointment stirred the crowd. People murmured among themselves, unsure what to expect. Nothing at all seemed to be happening.

And then the tattoo winked.

Louisa sucked in a breath, grabbing hold of the bench before she lifted off it. The crowd hushed once more. She might have thought it a trick of the light or a ripple of the man's muscle, but the other eye winked just then. The man turned a circle, ensuring everyone in the audience, even those in the very last row like Louisa, could see.

"Yes, I am just a man. But *she* is something special, is she not?"

When he referred to her, Lovely Valentine rolled her shoulders. She combed her fingers through her hair. And then she slunk across the man's white skin, slipping around the tattooed heart and up his arm to his collarbone, as if she were only walking here to there. When she reached his chest, she twirled, and then blew the audience a silent kiss.

And it was only because of the equally silent crowd, enthralled by the show, that Louisa heard the quiet, sneaking footsteps coming up behind her. She didn't have to turn; she knew it was the boy.

She stood abruptly, fleeing down the aisle. Although her feet skipped just over everyone's toes, her bag swung at her side. "Sorry, sorry," she whispered as heads swiveled and faces glared up at her for spoiling the show.

At the end of the row, she spared a backward glance. The boy sprinted forward. His eyes bore into her, determined and dangerous. Louisa felt a flutter of panic, as if one of those oversized butterflies resided in her chest.

Ducking low, she grabbed hold of the tent's dusty hem. She yanked and pulled, but the stakes held it securely in place.

The boy's footfalls came faster. Louisa tugged harder.

The material loosened just enough for her to fit, and she flattened herself as much as she could, shimmying her way through the gap without touching the ground. Even before she'd climbed to her feet, a hand reached out after her. She swung her bag, smacking the boy's fingers. A muffled yelp came from inside the tent, and his fingers disappeared.

For now.

Any moment he might scramble out from under the tent and drag her to the proprietors. It didn't matter that she hadn't hurt a thing. They'd punish her, no doubt, for sneaking over the fence.

Dashing back into the heart of the carnival, Louisa squared her shoulders. Though she longed to slip back to the tent and finish watching the show, she couldn't let anything distract her again.

But that was easier said than done, for no sooner had she passed the Spider's Web (without so much as glancing at the child gleefully jumping upon it) than she saw a prancing white horse with a woman standing atop it, and Louisa's jaw dropped in awe.

The crowd parted, drawing in a collective breath as the rider suddenly dipped down, brown hands splayed on the horse's back, and kicked her legs up into the air. And in this manner, balanced in a perfect handstand with pointed toes, the woman rode the pale mare until Louisa could no longer see them.

Louisa shook herself. She would need to approach her search for her father more purposefully; otherwise she risked being led astray by the next wondrous act she encountered, and the boy would again sneak up on her unaware . . . and then who knew what ill fate might befall her.

She looked over the faces of the nearest vendors, took a steadying breath, and when their eyes met, slipped over to the golden-haired, golden-dressed girl in the middle (who could not have been any older than Louisa). The girl working the cart wore a black-lipped smile, which stood in stark contrast to her pale face. Gold shimmered on her eyelids. She ran a string of shiny beads through her fingers, holding them out for Louisa to admire.

"Aren't these gorgeous?" The beads clicked together as the girl swung them back and forth. "Three coppers, is all."

"Yes, um, they're quite nice," Louisa said. "But I was hoping you might point me in the direction of . . ." Louisa faltered, not knowing how to put into words what she wanted to find.

"Oh, two coppers, then," the girl said. Maybe she'd thought Louisa was trying to bargain.

"I haven't enough money." Louisa's cheeks warmed. She glanced down so she did not have to see the inevitable look of sympathy (or worse—pity) slide across the girl's pretty-made face.

"Ah, I'm such a gob," the girl said.

Louisa pushed on. "I'm looking for the . . . air walking . . . show?"

"You mean the Wingless Raven?"

Of course, Louisa was not at all certain, but she nodded, filling with hope. Her father might very well have assumed this mysterious stage name for his airborne performance, for a raven's wing would be as dark as his hair. "Where?"

"Head thataway." The girl pointed down the lane. "Can't miss it if you look up."

8

A TERRIBLE DARKNESS

Louisa darted forward, worried about the boy somewhere behind her, but hopeful, *so hopeful*, for what
might lie before her.

Her arms swung at her sides with renewed expectation
as she neared a crowd of people with their heads tilted back.
From where she stood, she could not yet glimpse what had
captured their attention, but her pulse quickened.

She stepped around and past the people in her way,
until she reached a sign (vertical this time) with a long
arrow pointing toward the heavens. It read:

Wingless Raven: Night–Rope Walker

Louisa took a deep breath, lifting an extra inch off the
ground, and touched the sign. All eyes focused skyward, so
no one noticed how her toes tickled the air.

"Father," she whispered. Could it really be him? Those

old black-and-white photographs were the closest to her father she'd ever come. Until now. She thought of letting herself rise higher, greeting him midair, and flinging herself into his arms. But she tempered her excitement and her carelessness.

Slowly, so she could hold on to the possibility just a little longer, she tipped back her head. The sky looked endless, so dark above and glittering with stars. She shivered. For so long she'd thought her father was lost among them, but now she swelled with hope that he might be within reach.

It was all she saw at first, the wide, wide night. But then a figure, still at a distance, came into view. More shadow than person, it glided through the air. Like a dark ghost.

And then, quite impossibly, the figure leaned to the side, body held straight, until it stood parallel to the horizon. Louisa's head spun, as if the world itself had tilted. Walking forward again, the figure continued its rotation, turning like the hands of a clock, and floated through the air upside down for several seconds before righting itself once again.

In the crowd, a frightened child tucked his face into his mother's side, but all Louisa could do was stare. Her heart pounded so loudly that the many sounds of the carnival—the music, the laughter, the chatter—dimmed. She wanted to spin into the air and walk through the night in a way she never had before, but she remained where she was, mindful of her promise to her mother.

Besides, the figure above graced the sky in the very way Louisa could not—nimble and sure-footed, unafraid of all the watching eyes.

Closer and closer, the Wingless Raven came, traveling a perfectly straight line. So perfect, in fact, that Louisa suddenly realized an impossibly long rope was strung from one tent pole to another. And the Wingless Raven walked across it.

Louisa let out a breath, feeling deflated. Her father would have no need for a rope. Like Louisa, he needed only breath and air to scale the sky.

Passing just above her now, the Wingless Raven slipped even more clearly into view. The black tights and feathered leotard, the slender brown arms and rounded hips, the dark hair tossing in the wind. It could not possibly be her father, for the Wingless Raven was a woman.

Louisa clasped her hands to keep them from trembling. She'd been silly to think it would be so simple to find him. Her father could be *anywhere*.

All the sounds of the carnival came crashing back, and with them came the tick, tick, tick of the love bugs' creeping legs. Louisa hardened her heart, pushing back a disappointment so heavy it threatened to crush her. She stomped her foot, for all the good it did, as it punished the air, not the ground. The love bugs fled.

Only, they may not have been frightened off by Louisa.

From nowhere, a terrible darkness encroached. It circled up from the dirt, surrounding her and no one else. Shadows pressed in from all sides. One moment, she was looking at the sky, and the next moment, absolute blackness surrounded her.

Cold fingers closed around her wrist. She tried to pull away, but the hand tightened its grip, dragging her forward.

⸂ 9 ⸃
UNMOORED

Louisa struggled hopelessly. Her legs slugged along, numb down to her toes, like they didn't belong to her. It was the same heavy feeling she'd had when the boy grabbed her ankle and tugged her from the air.

"Let me go," she said.

"I won't," the boy, just to the left of her, replied gruffly. "You'll run off."

"Doesn't do any good to run," came a familiar voice at her right. A girl's voice. Beads clacked together, just as they had when that golden-haired vendor had tried to sell them. "We'll only hunt you down again."

"Quiet," a second girl snapped with a tone so sharp and whip-like that Louisa bit her tongue and remained silent.

They continued on without another word. Still Louisa could not see, and her body felt like stone, so the boy was forced to lug her along. The hum of the crowd grew muffled, as if they were taking her to a neglected corner of the carnival to cage her with animals while they alerted the authorities. And once they arrived, there would be no hiding her floating.

Louisa's heart pounded, ready to leap out of her chest. Wherever they were taking her, they marched there purposefully, without pause or hesitation. When they finally stopped, Louisa's heart thumped faster still.

Her three captors mumbled to one another. All Louisa could hear was the first girl whispering, ". . . tied up . . ."

Louisa flinched at the thought of her arms and legs being bound. She could stay quiet no more. "I'll scream," she warned, filling her lungs and readying her cry.

"Try it," said the second girl.

Louisa opened her mouth, but as soon as she did, the darkness over her eyes spread over her lips as well. Her scream burst forth, but it was a muffled, near-silent noise.

"Mercy," said the boy, as if he'd taken some pity on Louisa.

Suddenly, the darkness lifted up and away from Louisa's eyes and her mouth. She blinked, and the webbed darkness that had surrounded her spooled in the air and then melded with the shadows. She swiped her free hand across her face, worried some swath of darkness still touched her.

"What was that?" she gasped.

Two awful girls and one horrible boy stood before her.

"A blindfold," said the girl with the whip-like voice. Silver barrettes pinned her dark hair up in a messy array, and black, shimmery powder circled her eyes like a masquerade mask.

"So you couldn't see," said the bead seller, which seemed rather obvious to Louisa. Although she didn't really know this girl with the black-painted lips, gold-sparkled eyelids, and string of shiny beads, Louisa felt a pinch of betrayal after their friendly first encounter.

"So you couldn't *run*," the boy said, looking pointedly at Louisa.

Oh, but she wanted to. Her eyes skipped all around, taking in her surroundings. A few feet away stood a spindly maple with squash-colored leaves. Beneath it hunkered a small carnival tent, the black-and-gold stripes faded, the gap between the curtains glowing with a sinister light. She did not want to meet who they'd brought her to.

Louisa tried to twist her arm from the boy's grasp, but he was very strong despite his skinny bones. "Out of my way." Louisa put as much force into the words as she could, but even she heard the uncertainty in her voice.

The boy narrowed his golden eyes. Louisa was happy to note that dirt smudged his coat and even his cheek, likely collected when he'd squirmed under the tent's flap chasing after her.

At last, the boy sighed and dropped Louisa's wrist. Instantly, she felt more like herself, a thousand times lighter. But with the horrible boy glaring at her, she knew she needed to escape before the trio changed their minds and turned her in.

Louisa glanced behind her: at the barb-wrapped fence, at the Spark Woods, at the folds of darkness. "I'm . . . I'm leaving." Her voice wavered before she could steady it.

Not that she had any idea where to go. She'd pinned so many hopes on what she might find at the carnival, and now she felt unmoored. And alone.

"But you've only just arrived!" said the girl with the beads. She sprang forward, the strand outstretched in her hands, and looped it around Louisa's neck quite unexpectedly.

Startled, Louisa ran her fingers over the beads, as if the gift of them might be some trick. But they looked and felt perfectly ordinary.

"Why did you run?" the boy asked. He scrubbed a hand over his face, but the smudge of dirt remained.

"I thought—" Louisa looked back and forth between them, confused. "I thought you meant to tie me up."

The boy snorted.

"No, we said, 'She's tied up.' As in *busy*. And we weren't referring to you," the dark-haired girl said. "You're more of a gob than Jess," she added, jutting her head toward the bead seller.

"I am not." Louisa didn't know what a gob was, but she didn't much like the sound of it. But better she be called a silly name than any of the other horrors she'd imagined.

Jess's black-painted lips split into a smile. She giggled. "'Course you're not. Just look at you."

Four pairs of eyes glanced down at Louisa's feet. Somehow, she'd managed to drift several inches off the ground. "Oh no," she said. Although the boy had already seen her do so, she felt exposed with all of them watching her.

"I told you, Mercy. That's how she got over the fence so fast." The boy's frown disappeared, replaced with a smile Louisa didn't understand.

Jess clapped her hands together. "Wish I could fly."

"I can't *fly*," Louisa said.

"What can you do, then?" Mercy's voice was less sharp now and more curious.

"What can *you* do?" Louisa asked, as they'd shown some unusual abilities of their own. And if they really didn't mean to start some sort of trouble, they might understand what it meant to be so very different.

"Ox is stronger than anyone," Jess said with pride.

Strong the Ox: Boy Beast

Louisa's eyes widened. She never would have guessed it. He was a stick of a boy. Yet with his golden eyes, his pointed incisors, and his grip like a vise, she could not help but believe it. (Although he made for a rather scrawny beast.)

"Last year, he mangled the fence. Tore right through it to get into the carnival," Jess added.

"And Mercy"—Ox thrust his thumb toward the girl with dark hair—"arrived not long after that."

Mercy smiled, her mouth a thin slip. She lifted her hand, wiggled her bony fingers. A mist of darkness pressed close around the group. "The shadows smuggled me in."

Louisa had always shied away from shadows, but this girl let them swarm around her. Louisa took a step back, a wisp of fear crawling along her spine as she realized who stood before her. A girl able to command the shadows. A girl who spun webs.

Merciless the Spider: Shadow Spinner

"Oh my!" Louisa's hand covered her mouth.

Mercy laughed, a scratchy, almost silly sound. "Shadows can't hurt you."

"I know." All the same, Louisa remembered how they'd nestled close to her mother, darkening the hollows of her cheeks.

The other girl, Jess, cleared her throat. They turned to her. She looked at Ox, as if waiting to be properly introduced.

"Jess sneaked into the carnival through a broken section of the fence," he said with a shrug.

Jess's hands shot to her hips. She cleared her throat again.

"Oh, right," Ox said while Mercy snickered. "Jess stole into the carnival like a dastardly thief in the night."

Jess beamed.

"Cut up her hands, though," Mercy added.

"The seamstress healed them all right." Jess held her hands toward the moonlight. Small silver scars glinted on her palms. She looked at Louisa. "No magic in me, but the carnival still let me in."

"What do you mean? How can a carnival let someone in?" Louisa thought of the ticket, how it'd appeared out of nowhere and disappeared just as suddenly, blown over the fence and teasing her to follow.

Ox folded his arms. "That's what we've been trying to tell you—"

"Ah," a voice creeped out from the tent. "The little levitationist has arrived."

ᖗ 10 ᖘ
THE MISFORTUNE TELLER

L ouisa's heart leaped in her throat, and she, Ox, Mercy, and Jess spun around all at once.

A beautiful woman with skirts layered moss, turquoise, and amber stood by the tent beneath the spindly maple. The pale strands of her long hair waved in the breeze. "Come," she said, and then turned abruptly, sweeping into the tent.

Louisa stared after her. As if the evening had not already surprised and dazzled her enough, what with the incredible feats she'd seen and her shadowy snatching, seeing the flower vendor here at the carnival nearly knocked Louisa off her feet. Her appearance seemed too much a coincidence.

Unless she had only imagined it was the flower vendor. After all, Louisa had seen her so briefly, and tonight, she'd let her imagination run quite wild.

"Well, go on, then." Jess elbowed Louisa once, then twice, before Louisa took a hesitant step forward.

A length of vine had wrapped itself around a stake holding up a small sign, one Louisa hadn't noticed until she drew closer. The board was simple and unadorned, the words as faded as the old tent. She swallowed hard when she read it.

Fiona All-Seeing: Misfortune Teller

She had never heard of such a thing. It was no wonder this tent was tucked so far back from the others, as Louisa could not think of who might want to hear of their misfortunes. It seemed a terrible thing to know. What good would it be, knowing of hardship before it happened, if there was nothing to be done about changing it?

"We'll wait here," Ox said. The tent's flaps swayed in the breeze, but it almost looked like fingers held them back.

"She means to welcome you, not bite you." Mercy stirred up the shadows, sending them swirling around Louisa's ankles, as if to scare her forward.

With the still-raw ache of her mother's passing, Louisa couldn't bear hearing if other misfortunes were to befall her. Although, she supposed, nothing could be worse than what she had already lost, so with a determined step she snubbed the love bugs and marched through the tent's dark opening.

Inside, it felt considerably warmer, but that might have had more to do with the nerves tingling through Louisa's body than the temperature. A flush ran up her neck as she looked at her surroundings.

Glass-contained fire hung glowing from the pole-spined roof. Everywhere, vines twisted. They ran up the walls of the tent and spread across the dirt floor. Some even poked tiny holes through the tent's fabric. A collection of them dripped down from above, portioning off a corner of the tent, perhaps to separate working and living quarters. In the center of the room sat a table and two chairs, cloaked in greenery.

The woman (it *was* the flower vendor—she even wore a red rose behind her ear) stood to the side and ran gentle dusk-colored fingers over the leaves. They unfurled at her touch, rustling and whispering. She turned to Louisa with that familiar smile, somewhere between appraisal and warmth.

"Won't you sit down? Have a seat? Take a chair?"

Louisa stepped forward and pulled out the chair as gently as she could so as not to tear the vines twined around its legs. She set down her bag. The woman sat across from her, arranging her skirts neatly.

"What are you called?"

"Louisa." It had been so long since anyone had cared to ask that her name stuck in her throat. "Louisa LaRoche."

"I'm Fiona Dior," said the woman, confirming what the sign outside the tent had announced.

Although she'd felt overly warm only moments before,

a chill sent goose bumps racing along her arms. "A teller of misfortunes?"

"Yes. Of sorts." She spoke as if she'd had to explain this idea many times before. "It is like the heads and tails of a coin. Toss it into the air and chance determines how it falls, which side faces up, which down. I see one side of a coin, but that doesn't mean we can forget about the other."

"Oh," Louisa said, not sure she understood completely.

"Think of it like this. Fortune brought you to the carnival; you sneaked past the very fabric of magic surrounding it. Isn't that so misfortunate for all the other places you might have visited?"

"I suppose so."

Fiona's eyes darkened. "I'm pleased you accepted the invitation I left you, Louisa. You seemed so sorrowful." She glanced down, where, beneath the table, Louisa's feet hovered just above the ground. "And so special."

"*Strange*, you mean," Louisa said, flinching as she recalled the dark looks aimed her way in the square.

"That too," Fiona immediately agreed, as if it was something wondrous to behold.

And maybe it was. Like Lovely Valentine. Like Wingless Raven. Even like Merciless the Spider, though Mercy's magic was darker than the others and creepy to be sure.

"Won't you join us? Share your talents? Use your gifts?" Fiona leaned forward as she spoke, firelight glinting in her eyes.

Louisa hesitated, stunned that she'd met someone who thought floating a talent, one to be exhibited. It tempted her greatly, but a stronger hope still curled inside her—the idea that she might come to know, that she might *find*, her father. But her search of the carnival had turned up empty, so surely he must be somewhere else? She refused to accept that he might be lost forever in the forest of stars. The carnival had to be a stepping-stone to reaching him.

Fiona's next string of questions broke into Louisa's thoughts. "Am I mistaken? Are you well taken care of? Have you a warm, loving home?"

Fiona must have known that wasn't true, not anymore, but Louisa could not bring herself to admit it. "Did you leave an invitation for the others? For Ox and Jess and Mercy?"

"Yes." A slow smile slid across Fiona's lips. "Though, I don't like to tip fortune too much in any one direction. It was up to them to determine what to do with the invitation. Just as it's your choice to make. And your fortune to follow."

"It was not fortune that brought me here, but misfortune," Louisa admitted darkly. A tremor ran through her voice at the thought of her mother resting forever beneath the earth, one small stone and wilted daises marking her grave.

"Sometimes that is the way of it."

A silence filled the space between them. Louisa guessed that Fiona was waiting—waiting for Louisa to accept her offer to join the carnival, for her to put her strange abilities to good use. "Thank you for your offer." Louisa straightened her shoulders, not sure what she would say until the words left her mouth. "I cannot stay."

"I'm sorry to hear it." Fiona spoke as if she had expected it, but Louisa reasoned that it must be very difficult to surprise someone who could read misfortunes. "At the very least, stay through the night. It's much too late to travel the woods alone. Ox and the others will show you around."

"Okay." Louisa was quick to agree. She needed to think things through. She needed to find the next stepping-stone. Her father could be anywhere in the whole of the world.

"Before you run off, shall I tell your misfortune?"

Louisa's heart beat fast, quite unnecessarily, she thought. But she could not calm it. "I'd rather not know."

Fiona cocked her head. "Are you certain?"

For all the hesitation she'd had entering the tent and for all the doubt she'd felt about seeking misfortunes, when the question lay before her, Louisa realized she wasn't certain at all. Instead, a dark curiosity gripped her. Maybe it was better to be prepared for what was to come.

Or maybe Fiona would tell her something about where her father was.

"Well . . . ," Louisa said.

Fiona's smile grew wide. As she'd done in the square, when Louisa knew her as no one other than the flower vendor, Fiona tore a petal off the rose in her hair and rubbed it between her fingers.

Louisa did not know the ways of fortune-telling, although she had imagined futures foretold in the bottom of teacups or at the turn of three tarot cards, but Fiona touched none of the peculiar items on the table before her.

"Lean forward," Fiona said. "Let me see your eyes."

Louisa did as she was told, blinking them wide, wondering what could be seen in them beyond their blue coloring.

The misfortune teller gazed into their depths the way she might have peered into a crystal ball. It was rather unsettling, having so much attention directed on her, and Louisa shifted in her seat, looking away when Fiona frowned.

"Is it that terrible?" Louisa asked.

Fiona paused. "It might be." The rose petal fell from her fingers to the floor. It was sapped of color, gone as gray as Louisa's stone heart. Before Louisa could change her mind, before she could ask Fiona to keep the misfortune to herself, Fiona said, "You will never find who you are looking for."

11

MAGIC, MARVELS & MYSTIQUES

Louisa sucked in a breath, dismayed and angry and confused all at once. Her chair tipped back, falling to the floor as she floated several inches into the air.

"My!" Fiona exclaimed. "How little mastery you have."

Louisa exhaled slowly, tempering her emotions and her breath, and then righted the chair. But she did not take her seat again.

"How did you know—" Her voice broke and she started again. "How did you know I was looking for someone?" It was a silly thing to ask. Fiona must have seen misfortunes the way Louisa's feet never touched the ground—because neither of them could help it. The magic was a part of them, same as the shades of their skin and the colors of their eyes.

It wasn't the question Louisa wanted to ask anyway. No,

those questions she bit back. They were too wrapped up inside her, too close to her heart.

But they echoed in her head.

Is it true? Will I never find him?

Will I be alone forever?

"Your eyes." Fiona stood. Her skirts rippled like waves. "Your eyes shared your misfortune. They told me this truth."

Louisa blinked, wishing she could look into them and uncover the secrets stored inside her. Maybe then she would not feel so lost.

"But remember, like a coin, there are two sides to this misfortune. Will you consider what I could not see? What only you can see? What your heart tells you?"

Louisa let the rhythm of these fast words roll through her. "I will try," she said.

"Who is it you seek?"

"My father."

Fiona nodded sympathetically. She reached a hand to her hair, running fingers through the pale strands, and then plucked a lock from her head. It curled, it grew, it blossomed. A daisy rested in her palm. She bent down, tucking it behind Louisa's ear.

"Tell me about him."

After witnessing such a strange sort of magic, it took Louisa a moment to gather herself. She touched the soft petals of the magicked flower. As much as it amazed her, it also comforted her—this small reminder of her mother—and gave her the courage to speak.

"His name is William LaRoche," she said, digging out her photographs and passing them to Fiona. She repeated what her mother had told her about his work as a stage-hand, about his sketches (of which her mother hadn't saved a single one).

"He has hair as black as a starless midnight sky—like mine—and he walks through the air instead of stepping on the ground. But he floated away long ago." Louisa stopped there, realizing how little she knew of him. Not enough to properly describe him. "I *will* find him," she added, defiant of her misfortune, for she would not give up when she'd only just begun.

Fiona showed no signs of recognizing the name or the bare description or the blurry image in any of the photographs. "Your father may have come here once." Fiona tapped the photograph of Louisa's parents in front of the striped tent. "But only in passing. I do not recognize him. He isn't among us now." She offered no false assurances; she only smiled bleakly, and then lifted her eyes, looking at something behind Louisa.

A throat cleared.

Louisa spun round. Crowded into the tent's entrance stood Ox, Jess, and Mercy. They'd heard everything she'd said of her father. A stretch of silence passed. Ox looked at the ground, Mercy chewed her lip, and Jess stepped closer, taking Louisa by the hand.

"Come on. It's time for one of my favorite shows." Jess tugged Louisa forward.

"B-but," Louisa stammered. "My bag—"

Mercy curled a shadow around Louisa's other hand—it felt like smoke, tickling her palm—and together with Jess, they pulled Louisa from the tent. Ox walked beside them, head down, quiet despite the girls' excitement.

The other girls, that is. Louisa could not be swept up in their delight. Her misfortune still thundered in her head.

"We'll be too late to get good seats," Jess moaned.

"I'll sneak us backstage." Mercy snugged a shadow close around them, not too thick; Louisa could still gaze through it, but perhaps everyone else would struggle to see them behind it.

"What show?" Louisa asked as they rushed her along, overwhelmed and wanting only to be left alone as she was used to.

Neither girl answered, perhaps too busy plotting how they would slip into the tent. Louisa turned to Ox. His hair had fallen into his eyes, but she could see their golden glow when he glanced up at her. But he did not answer her either. Without so much as touching it, his hair swept back from his face.

"How—" Louisa began, but Ox stalked ahead of the group, quite rudely ignoring her.

So, with no one bothering to tell her, it was the sign that announced the show. As they whisked past it, Louisa read the black lettering.

Fire-Red Rosalyn: Igniter of the Spark Woods

Hushing them, Mercy tightened the shadows around the group and herded everyone into the tent, right under the nose of the burly carnival worker at the rear entrance. Jess looked on the verge of breaking into laughter. From the darkness, an extra shadow wrapped itself around her mouth, which Mercy kept firmly in place. Jess yanked at it to no avail.

They smooshed close together as Louisa peered past the curtain. Rosalyn had already taken the stage.

She wore a sparkling leotard of orange and red. Each time she moved, it glinted. With a collective breath, the audience gazed up at her. Their mouths dropped open as she exhaled fire and then licked each of her fingers with a fiery tongue. As she did so, a bright orange flame jumped at each tip.

In that moment, Louisa had quite forgotten about her desire to be left alone. Her sadness, still present, at least quieted.

With each finger alight, Rosalyn ran her hands through her hair. Her skin was the color of the earth, and against it, her long, brown locks blazed like a sunset, rippling with spark and flame. She fisted her hands, smothering the fire on her palms, and then reached skyward for an aerial ring that lowered from the roof of the tent. Once she had secured her grip, the ring rose higher and higher. In the crowd, all heads tipped back. Rosalyn flipped over and around the ring, and then set it spinning.

Her fiery hair streaked wild with each rotation. Sparks flew from the strands and showered down on the audience.

A sense of magic tingled in the very air.

Louisa gasped.

The carnival worker they'd skirted past snapped his head to the side. He squinted at the shadows. "Mercedes, is that you?" he hissed under his breath. "You know you're not supposed to be back here." He swiped a hand through the air, but Mercy stood well out of reach.

Shadows swarmed closer, shading Louisa's view. She held them back just long enough to see the rain of fire extinguish spark by spark before it reached the crowd. Then Mercy's shadow magic wrapped Louisa and the rest of them in darkness. Beyond it, the audience roared with applause.

Something pulled Louisa from behind, a force she could not resist. No one touched her, she was sure of it, but a great weight clamped onto each limb, the same heaviness as when Ox had grabbed her boot and pulled her from the air. A whisper of laughter bounced within the shadow, close to her ear. She felt herself propelled backward and into the night.

Moments later, the shadows dispelled. As quickly as it had come, the weight lifted.

They stood at a distance to the tent where Fire-Red Rosalyn still performed. Jess giggled, Mercy smiled like she'd gotten away with something, and Ox was already walking away from them.

Louisa shook her arms and legs, flicking off the strange sensation that had come over her. Whether or not she had felt his hand, it must have only been Ox, yanking her from the tent by the sleeve of her coat. She watched him go.

"What's wrong with him?" Mercy asked, as if she was disappointed he hadn't been impressed with her sneakiness.

"Never mind him for now. I'm starving," Jess said, and with that, she led Louisa and Mercy forward.

Louisa might have gone after Ox to confront him if only she had not been so sorely hungry. "Is he acting like a gob?" She wondered if she was using the word correctly.

Jess erupted in laughter and looped her arm through Louisa's. "Most certainly!"

The three of them wove in and out of the crowds. "What *is* a gob?" Louisa asked.

"Someone like me," Jess said. "Someone without any magic. Like, a silly, oblivious goblin." She smiled, all teeth and black-painted lips, as if she quite liked the name, despite the absence of magic.

"Magic," Louisa said. Never before had she considered *floating* to be magical, but it felt right. It felt better than thinking of herself as a freak. "Is that what this carnival is made of?"

"Oh yes," Jess said. "The very best sorts of magic."

"Tell me more," Louisa begged.

"Better yet, let me show you," Mercy said. "Hold out your hand."

Louisa did as she was told, and Mercy swirled her fingers through the air, calling the shadows. One wispy swath snaked away from all the others. It settled in Louisa's palm, twisting and darkening at Mercy's command like a cold, black flame.

"That's magic. Controlling something else, like I do with the shadows or Rosalyn does with fire."

Louisa stared at the shadow in frightened awe.

"You can keep it," Mercy said. "In case you need it."

"Um," Louisa said, hesitant. "Thank you." Any other response would have been rude. Very carefully, she tucked the shadow into the pocket of her coat.

"Oh!" Jess exclaimed. "But that's not all. Look there." She pointed ahead of them to where the pale mare Louisa had spied earlier pranced along, its graceful rider balancing on its back. "That's a marvel. Mastering a talent, like acrobatics or playing an instrument."

"How wondrous," Louisa said.

"Don't you mean how *marvelous*?" Jess laughed and laughed.

Mercy elbowed Jess quiet and with her dark-ringed eyes looked straight at Louisa. "And then there's you, controlling something within yourself."

"Magic?" Louisa asked.

"Something rarer," Mercy confided, voice dark, as if she offered a secret. "You're a mystique."

❧ 12 ❧
THE MARIONETTE & THE SEAMSTRESS

Louisa asked for a moment to herself. All the lights and sights of the carnival, all of Jess's and Mercy's chatter, and then this latest revelation—it made her head spin. They left her in a quiet corner of the carnival well away from the crowds, promising to bring back supper.

But a different sort of hunger stirred in her belly. Fiona had declared that one path in Louisa's life was closed, the path that would lead to her father. Louisa refused to believe the misfortune teller, but even still, it felt like another path had opened before her. She looked down at her feet and the space beneath them. A mystique!

She thought the name lovely.

With a wistful sigh, she touched the daisy in her hair, wishing she could share this moment with her mother, when at last she had a name for her strange gift. One that sounded extraordinary—not dangerous, not something to hide. Louisa, so used to deflecting notice, had the sudden desire to show off.

Maybe she still could.

Louisa looked left and right, ensuring she stood alone. And then, with a deep, controlled breath, she lifted into the air. "Watch this," she whispered, hoping her mother was listening and watching from the beyond. "Look what I can do." More purposefully than she'd ever done before, Louisa spun herself around. She twirled in a circle, the skirt of her dress rippling, the toes of her boots defying gravity.

Although she wasn't entirely graceful, she was entirely pleased with herself, and rose a little higher. She reached for the string of glass orbs hanging above.

"There you are," a voice whispered from the gloom.

"Who's there?" Louisa bobbled in the air. She exhaled a breath, trying to lower herself to the ground, but as usual, she had more trouble on the descent and hovered there, arms out like useless wings. She peered into the spaces between the tents.

A figure walked through the night. In sharp contrast to the softness of his voice, a great heaviness weighted each lumbering step. From the stomping of his boots, she expected someone much bigger, but though he stood tall, his angular body was thin and long limbed. He wore a pair of black pants and a jacket of striped black and gold, fashioned in the same manner as the carnival's tents. A blood-red square of fabric popped up from the front pocket of his coat. On his head rested a top hat, though it looked like he'd sat upon it once, as the sides crinkled, and it wobbled a bit—accordion-like—as he approached.

When he stepped fully into the light, Louisa shrank back in fright. He loomed above her, his face a strange construction of skin—some smooth and pale, some rough and splintered—and then tipped his hat. Beneath it, his hair gleamed silver, as if it had been dunked in moonlight.

"Good evening," he said, looking at her rather crookedly, one eye blue and one eye brown.

He lurched closer. Firelight melted across his face, unmasking every feature.

Bits and pieces of the man were carved from wood.

He had a wooden jaw and a wooden cheek, and a wooden eye that stared and stared but never blinked.

"Here," he said softly, and reached out with one long arm. Something swung from the end of his fingers, three of which were made of skin and bone, the other two of wood.

"Oh." Louisa's cheeks warmed, recognizing her bag. Fiona must have asked him to bring it to her. "Thank you."

Their fingertips touched as she accepted her bag. No sooner did her hand close around the strap than she heard the clicking of the love bugs, still clinging to her things. She shook the bag, but they did not quiet.

The man seemed not to notice and turned to go. Before disappearing into the night, he glanced back at her. "With some practice, you will soar to the stars."

◁ ★ ▷

"Who is he?" Louisa asked Mercy and Jess once they had all settled down in a soft patch of leaves to eat.

"Quiet Si," Jess said around a mouthful of her sandwich. "The"—her chomping mumbled the next word—"Marionette."

Louisa chewed, deep in thought. "If he is a marionette, who is pulling his puppet strings?"

Jess wiped a hand over her lips, removing crumbs. Before she could speak, Mercy rolled her eyes and said, "No one. He is Quiet Si: The *Unstringed* Marionette."

"Oh." Louisa looked in the direction he had gone. Unstringed or not, the idea of being a marionette sounded rather frightening. She remembered the feeling she'd had in Fire-Red Rosalyn's tent, of something pulling her, something controlling her.

"He's odd for sure," Jess said. "No one can figure out exactly what he is."

"A marvel," Mercy said, as if she knew a truth no one else did. "He learns all he can of everyone's magic, and he trains us and helps to design our acts."

"A goblin," Jess said. "He has no more magic than me, just a spooky face that makes you think otherwise."

"There just must be some magic in him," Louisa said, sure they were both wrong but unable to explain why.

Jess shrugged, unconvinced. "Are you done eating? There's someone else who wants to meet you."

Louisa yawned. She would have been glad to curl up above the leaves and go to sleep right then and there.

But curiosity won out. "Who?"

"Come on."

Louisa followed Mercy and Jess around the edges of the carnival. As they approached a small tent with black, gold, *and* red stripes, a woman stepped from its folds, as if she'd been expecting them.

"Welcome." Her low voice swept through the night.

"Hello," Louisa said once they'd drawn closer.

The woman offered a slow, closed-mouth smile. In her fine-boned hands, she held a pair of knitting needles and a skein of yarn as vibrant as cardinal feathers. Her dress, long and wide-skirted, matched the color precisely. "I'm Darcelle Duval." The needles clicked against each other. "The Seamstress of the Carnival."

With her braided red hair spindled on top of her head

like the finest spool of thread and the fancy slippers on her feet, Darcelle Duval did not look the sort to darn socks or patch the knees of timeworn pants. Neither would she have sat, head bent, hemming an old, frayed skirt the way Louisa's mother had done.

Instead, Darcelle Duval must have made the feathered bodysuit worn by Wingless Raven, the glittering orange-flamed leotard donned by Fire-Red Rosalyn, the golden dress cinching Jess's waist, and even the strange striped suit belonging to Quiet Si.

Louisa imagined Darcelle Duval might very well have stitched the carnival into being.

Jess nudged Louisa, who hadn't meant to stare so obviously.

"This is Louisa LaRoche," Mercy introduced her.

"My mother was a seamstress." The words burst forth from Louisa, thoughts of her mother so, so close and needing release. "She taught me all she knew."

"Then we will have much to talk about," Darcelle said, and looked briefly to Mercy and Jess in turn. "Leave her with me. She will sleep here tonight."

"But I wanted her to see my show," Mercy grumbled. Around them, the sky darkened, as if she'd called many shadows at once.

"Oh, can't she stay with us?" Jess said, the plea heavy in her voice.

"We wouldn't want her to have nightmares, would we?" Darcelle raised one eyebrow at Mercy, then turned her attention to Jess. "I hear she is already leaving us come morning—"

"So soon?" Mercy cut in.

"She can't go yet," Jess insisted.

"It's her choice to make," Darcelle reminded them, and the girls bobbed their heads in reluctant acceptance. "And if she is to travel, she will need more sleep than either of you would allow her."

"All right," Jess said glumly, but before leaving she leaped forward and squeezed Louisa in a tight embrace. "Sleep well!"

"We'll see you tomorrow. And we'll drag Ox along with us, if we have to, and give you a proper goodbye then," Mercy said.

"Good night," Louisa called after them.

"Aren't they sweet." Darcelle watched them go, as if they might get up to some mischief, and then held back the curtain, allowing Louisa to proceed her into the tent.

Louisa froze in the entrance, eyes roving over her surroundings. She stood, not above a dirt-and-leaf floor, but above a tapestry of black, gold, and red. Every last slip of space was filled with the carnival's colors. Bolts of fabric lay in huge stacks; headless dress mannequins lined one wall, wearing gowns and costumes that shimmered in their elaborate design. Tall shelves held coils of ribbon, some half-unfurled and curling down to the floor, along with bottles and jars filled with sequins and glitter. A red crystal chandelier hung in the center of the tent, dripping with sheer crimson fabric that stretched along the ceiling like the petals of an enormous flower. The crystals glinted and tinkled like wind chimes.

Her mother would have loved to see it.

"It's beautiful," Louisa said, afraid to move and risk disturbing any of the materials.

"Here, let us sit." Darcelle strode into the tent and lowered herself gracefully onto a low pile of fabrics.

When Louisa joined her, Darcelle smiled again. It sat fragile on her face. Louisa expected her to ask about her mother or talk of her sewing marvel, but instead, the seamstress took up the yarn and her needles, looping and coiling without saying a word. It was nice, Louisa thought, just sitting there in the quiet. If she shut her eyes, she could have pretended the clicking of the needles was made by her mother's hands.

Darcelle touched her glossy red hair and plucked a stray silver strand from her scalp. She wound it around her needles, blending it with the yarn as she knit. It shone like tinsel, all glittery in the light. "Pretty, isn't it?"

"It's splendid," Louisa agreed.

Darcelle kept her eyes on her work. "Where will you go?"

Louisa ran her fingers over a golden scrap of fabric,

which must have been silk, it felt so soft. "Wherever the wind takes me," Louisa said, thoughts returning to her father.

"You are welcome to stay here with us, as I am sure Fiona told you. I could use another set of hands such as yours, skilled with a needle and thread." Darcelle gestured at the finery around them. "And more than that, the rest of the world does not understand magic and mystiques, or accept them, not as we do here—and we are always in need of *more*." Darcelle paused, as if Louisa might brighten at these remarks, change her mind and agree to stay, but Louisa had not been swayed by Fiona and neither would she be tempted by Darcelle.

"It is a kind offer."

Darcelle knit faster. "If you must go, then you might travel on to Northrup. This time of year, they hold a festival of the arts. Surely your father's floating is just one of his many talents. Might he have gone there to exhibit them?"

Louisa knew so little of her father and was about to say so, when snippets of her mother's stories drifted back to her—*that he was a night owl and sketched by the light of the moon, that he had once worked for the theater as a stagehand*. If he was not looking for the spotlight, he might be there, helping behind the scenes on a woodland performance or sketching patrons for a copper or two.

She leaned forward, eager to follow this next stepping-stone to her father. "How far is it?"

"It's the next town over. Straight north of here, through the Spark Woods." Darcelle paused, only long enough to wind another long, shiny strand of hair around her needles, and then, as if she'd read Louisa's mind, said, "Perhaps your father is there." She glanced up, and catching the hopeful look on Louisa's face, gently added, "But perhaps he is not. I should think I will see you again."

"Fiona told you of him?" Louisa asked, finding herself sinking back, resting just above the lovely fabrics. Almost, almost, she could feel them beneath her.

The needles clicked. "Yes."

"She told me I would not find him," Louisa admitted.

Darcelle's hands stilled, and she confided, "I'm afraid I must tell you that Fiona Dior's misfortunes are never wrong."

⌇ 13 ⌇
SHARING THE SILENCE

Louisa slept fitfully that night. She tossed atop the soft pile of fabrics, shaken, not by nightmares, but her unruly thoughts. She would travel to Northrup, but if her father wasn't there, she hadn't another stepping-stone in her path. Louisa released a weary sigh and opened her eyes.

Over the past lonely weeks, she'd grown so used to lying beneath the stars that when she saw the black, gold, and red stripes of the tent above her instead, she felt completely out of sorts and so very far from her mother.

But even in Plum, she would have been no closer. A gravestone marked only bones.

She rose from the small bed of fabric and reached for her things ever so quietly, so as not to wake Darcelle Duval, who breathed softly on the other side of the tent, deep in slumber. Lovingly folded atop Louisa's coat was a red knit scarf with fine threads of shimmering hair woven through it. Louisa could not believe Darcelle had completed it so quickly and so beautifully, and that she meant for Louisa to have it.

She pulled on her coat and lifted the scarf. It was so long she had to wrap it twice around her neck to keep it from dragging on the ground. Clutching her bag, she noiselessly slipped out of the tent, but not before stealing one last look at the seamstress, who lay with her red hair spilled around her, the soft waves like unspooled thread.

Outside, the air was crisp and the stars shone bright. There was just enough light to see by if she were to leave for Northrup right then. Though she'd readied herself for travel, she walked slowly forward, a contrary twist in her belly—she both wanted and did not want to leave. Saying goodbye to everyone might make it impossible.

Louisa slunk through the night, feeling a little like Mercy must, safe in the protection of the tents' looming shadows. Free to walk wherever she wanted, unseen.

Passing the shuttered carts and the closed-up tents, Louisa bundled her arms around herself. The carnival looked so different. Absent the crowds and the glow of the fiery glass orbs, it felt lonesome. *She* felt lonesome.

And yet, she did not feel as if she was *alone*.

In the quiet, she heard the softest footsteps behind her.

The entrance to the carnival arched just ahead. A few more strides and she would be gone. But she stopped. She turned.

A figure stood several feet behind her, and it was the last person she thought it might be. "Ox?"

With his rounded shoulders and frowning mouth, he looked especially troubled. "Are you leaving already?" His hair flopped into his face.

"Yes," she said, her heart clenching as she added, "there is nothing here for me."

She remembered floating among the stars the night before, and something within her whispered, *There could be. There might be.* Her hand went to the scarf Darcelle had gifted her. Against her chest lay the string of beads from Jess, and in her pocket rested the shadow from Mercy. And before her stood Ox.

But she could not give up on finding her father.

"I thought you'd stay." Invisible fingers seemed to reach out, brushing the hair from Ox's eyes. A soft autumn breeze must have swept by. But if so, it did not touch Louisa, for she lifted not even a bit into the air.

"Why are you following me?" Louisa asked, sure he hadn't wanted to talk to her the night before (although she didn't know why).

"I'm not following you. You're the one who passed by my tent." His eyes shown, reflective and bright. "And you are not as quiet as you think with all your sighing."

Louisa's hand flew to her mouth.

Ox's flash of annoyance passed as quickly as it had flared. "No one's ever left the carnival before, not when they've been invited to stay."

"No one?" Louisa asked. But it didn't really surprise her. It was a marvelous place, one that seemed almost too good to be true.

"No one." Ox shifted foot to foot. "And to be honest, I was following you."

"Oh?" Louisa did not know what to make of this boy with the golden eyes.

He stood there so long without response Louisa wondered if he would ever answer. And then he said, "My father died last year. I miss him." Ox toed the dirt and the leaves. "I hope you find yours."

Louisa had not expected his openness; neither had she expected to find someone who might understand her grief, and her desire to smother it. "I'm sorry," she said sincerely.

A small smile lifted the corners of his mouth. Sometimes the simplest sentiments were enough.

They said not another word for several moments, only stood there, side by side, watching the dwindling stars and sharing the silence.

"You don't have to go," Ox said finally. "I mean, not for good. Not forever."

"But my father—"

"This is a traveling carnival, you know. We go all over, and you could come with us."

"I can't," Louisa said automatically, but his idea poked around in her head, asking, *Why not, why not?*

"At least think about it," Ox said, and Louisa promised that she would.

◁ ★ ▷

Her first step away from the carnival felt like peering down from the edge of a very high cliff, unable to see all the way to the bottom. The unknown lay ahead. Oh, this time she would not pin *all* her hopes on finding her father in Northrup (only *most* of them), as her disappointment still sat heavily in her heart that he hadn't been at the carnival. But at least she had another stepping-stone on the path.

And Ox's offer circled in her head—that she might have a whole path of stones ahead.

A breeze swept close, toying with her scarf. The tufted ends whipped in the air and then fell still.

Louisa was usually cautious of the wind, but thoughts of her father occupied her so completely that she was hardly aware of her surroundings as she walked along. When Louisa neither looked up nor smoothed her flyaway hairs, the breeze strengthened, sweeping against the hem of her skirt so she could no longer ignore it.

Startled, Louisa glanced up.

The wind had stopped fussing with her clothes and now

tore leaves from the trees. A branch cracked in half and thundered to the ground. Louisa jumped, finally looking all around.

Threads of darkness spread through the woods, blotting out the road ahead.

And the road behind.

꞉ 14 ꞉
STRONG THE OX

Louisa stood in the middle of a storm, one unlike any she had seen before. Not a drop of rain fell. Not a single bolt of lightning streaked through the sky, which had been clear one moment and gone dark the next. The air tingled with electricity.

Or was it tingling with magic?

The feel of it—as wild as the flames at Fire-Red Rosalyn's fingertips, as sinister as Mercy's shadows, as unsettling as Fiona Dior's misfortunes—surrounded Louisa. She stared at the cloud of gray, so thick and so fast encroaching she didn't know which way to turn. Within it, the wind twisted alongside the darkness, tangling like the black ribbons and silver threads at the bottom of her mother's sewing basket.

The wind battered against her, and she fought to stay

grounded. She retreated, backing up slowly, exhaling, exhaling, exhaling just as her mother had taught her.

Louisa crouched low, her knees just above the ground, hoping the wind would sweep over and past—that it was only wind after all—but it gusted across her in warning. She ran her fingers through the crackling leaves, closing her hands around one small stone after another, and slipped them into the pockets of her coat until the material bulged.

The weight of the rocks reassured her. Their heaviness a promise to keep her closer to the earth.

Above, tree branches thrashed. Leaves spun like small tornadoes.

As if she weighed no more than one of those leaves, and despite the rocks in her pockets, Louisa tumbled up and into the air. Her feet went over her head, her arms flew out, and all the stones rained from her pockets to the ground. "No!" she cried, scrambling to keep hold of her bag.

But the wind fought the bag loose, and it fell.

Louisa only drifted higher. Tree branches swiped at her face and caught in her hair. The long strands snapped, and she shrieked. The wind—sharp as needle points on her face—took her where it wanted, as if she had no will of her own. She hoped her father had not felt this frightened, this helpless, when the wind came for him. She hoped he'd fought against it.

Another branch raked across her, ripping the sleeve of

her coat. Louisa reached out, grabbing hold of the branch's spiny tip. It splintered in her hand.

Louisa's muscles ached—how she pushed against the wind, how she fought her way closer to the tallest tree. If only she could reach its thick trunk—something solid to hold on to—she would not become lost in the magic-streaked sky.

She pushed the air from her lungs, a great release of her breath. Down she went, not by much, but enough to bring her nearer to the tree.

Pushing past leafless limbs, her hands scraped against bark. She dug her fingertips into the rough surface and wrapped her legs tight around the trunk. The wind circled, nudging against her, trying to tease her off. She pressed her cheek to the wood. She closed her eyes.

The storm will pass, she told herself, even if magically spun. If she just held on long enough she would be fine. Only, bit by bit, her fingers slipped against the bark, and her trembling legs grew weak. With a sudden whoosh, the wind ripped her away from the tree. Again, she tumbled through the air. Her head felt a blur.

Had her father flailed in such a manner? Had he seen the world pass beneath him upside down? Louisa did not want to blow away like he had, never to be seen again.

Her hand flew to her rippling scarf. She threw one long end of it, imagining it a lasso and aiming for the treetops.

The threads of wind lashed it away.

Still spinning, still dizzy, she gathered the scarf as best she could and then tossed it forward with all her might. It touched the branches; it snagged on the twigs. She felt the snap of the yarn as it stretched and grew taut.

And held.

She bobbed in the gray sky, the scarf her tremulous anchor.

◁ ★ ▷

Long moments passed. She thought she might never find her way to the ground.

"Louisa!" From below, someone called her name.

"Louisa!" Two more voices joined the first.

She stared into the distance. Through the branches and leaves, through the wild wind still circling, three figures ran down the road. She'd known them only a day, but she would have recognized them anywhere—Jess, Mercy, and Ox. Their heads swiveled all around as they peered into the woods and shouted her name.

"I'm here!" she cried.

At the base of the tallest maple, they stopped all at once and then turned their eyes to the sky. Louisa waved one arm, holding tight to the scarf with the other.

Ox waved back, as if it was all a silly game, like scaling the fence and stealing into the carnival. "What are you doing up there?" he called, unable to keep from grinning.

"Quick, quick! Get her down before she blows away," Jess said, shaking Ox's arm.

When he only stared up at Louisa, Mercy scrambled around the trunk, reached for the lowest branch, and swung up into the tree. *Spiderlike,* Louisa could not help but think, as if she were stuck in Mercy's web.

"Be careful!" Jess bit her fingernails.

"Please hurry," Louisa said at the same time. The unnatural storm whipped against her, skating right over the heads of Ox and Jess with only the lightest of tousles to their hair.

The branches grew thinner the closer Mercy came to Louisa, until they bent and creaked under her weight, warning her she should go no farther. Yet Mercy continued on, boot lifted, hand grasping. But there was still so much distance between them.

A determined wind rattled the branches, and before Mercy could secure her footing, it knocked hard against her. Her shoulder hit the trunk.

She screamed, wide-eyed. Her hand reached out. Her fingertips grazed the scarf wrapped around the spindly branch.

But they did not catch hold.

"No!" Louisa shouted, frantically trying to lower herself.

Mercy fell in slow motion.

At the same time, Louisa's chest tightened. A strange but familiar heaviness took hold of her limbs, and quite unexpectedly, she found herself floating down beside Mercy. Their arms hung at their sides, and around their legs, their skirts puffed up like black umbrellas suddenly popped open.

It was the most graceful descent Louisa had ever made, and one she could take no credit for.

Mercy landed gently on the ground. Louisa hovered at her side, the weight lifting from her once again. Ox grinned even wider.

Louisa thought back to the first time they'd met and the heaviness of his grip on her ankle. She thought of the way some force had drawn her from Fire-Red Rosalyn's tent and the way Ox's hair swept from his eyes without his needing to lift a hand. "It was you?"

"Of course it was him." Mercy glared at Ox, dusting bits of leaf and bark from her coat. "Though you might have offered a hand *sooner*."

"I forgot you haven't seen his show," said Jess. "We told you he was strong. He can lift anything."

Louisa's scarf, tangled in the tree's highest branches, suddenly twirled through the air and danced toward her. With a flip of its tassels, it settled on her shoulders, and then wrapped itself twice around her neck.

Ox tapped his head. "I lift things with my mind."

Louisa gaped at him. Whether with his thoughts or his hand, she'd felt the very weight of his magic each time he'd touched her, in such opposition to her own light-as-air bones. "Remarkable."

Mercy rolled her eyes, muttering, "Well, you're certainly not lifting things with your scrawny muscles."

Louisa might have smiled, but she wasn't out of danger just yet. "This storm is strange," she began, unsure if they felt its magical trembling as she did.

"Fiona thought so too. She was going on and on about doom and misfortune." Jess picked up Louisa's bag and held it out uncertainly. "You're coming with us, aren't you?"

The cold, prickly wind threaded between them.

Louisa looked down the road toward Northrup where the sky stormed black. The city would still be there tomorrow, waiting for her when she was ready. And when the way was not so menacing.

"Yes, I'm coming back with you." She accepted her bag from Jess, who linked their arms together.

The threads of the storm twisted closer, hurrying them most ominously along.

↳ 15 ↴
WAITING & WATCHING

The carnival sat in a patch of pale autumn sunshine, the tents' golden stripes gleaming, but something about the skyline did not look quite right. A thread of darkness cut across the horizon, as if the storm brewed here too, but more quietly.

Ox opened the gate at the front entrance, and Louisa slipped in after him and the others. Before them lay a very different carnival than the one Louisa had left the night before.

Leaves cluttered the pathway before them, alongside broken twigs, scraps of torn fabric, slivers of glass, and other odds and ends swept from the vendors' carts. As for the tents, long gashes ran down the sides of some. Beams collapsed inward on others. The big top was missing its roof entirely.

"Oh no," Louisa said. She touched the small tear on the sleeve of her coat, which seemed such an insignificant thing now, realizing how much worse off she might be if Mercy, Jess, and Ox had not come for her.

"The storm hit here first, fast and fierce, and then chased after you," Mercy said when she saw Louisa's dismayed expression.

Louisa folded her arms around her stomach. Yes. Yes, that was exactly how it had felt. As if the wind had come for her. Intentionally. Magically.

Maliciously.

No wonder her mother had always reminded her to be so careful. The world must have many types of magic, and not all of it good.

But Louisa was back at the carnival now, surrounded by so many kind faces, away from the strange magic that must have resided in the woods. She pushed back her fear as best she could. Nothing would harm her here.

"We thought you'd blow away for sure." Jess squeezed Louisa's arm. "You could have been headed to Northrup for the Fall Festival only to find yourself in Wilshire at the annual Pig Roast."

Ox snickered, but Jess continued. "It's dangerous for you out there alone."

All Louisa could think about was the truth of Jess's words. There were so many carnivals and circuses, festivals and fairs in the world (and roasts too, apparently), and she had no means to reach them all, not even if she spent her whole life looking. Especially not when the wind—and most especially that *ominous* wind—could so easily toss her about. Ox's idea to travel with the carnival once it was ready to move on from the Spark Woods sounded safer than going on her own, and it would give her time to manage her magic before she set off again.

From the heart of the carnival, heavy footsteps approached. Quiet Si, wearing his crinkled top hat and striped jacket, walked in a straight line toward them. Although he had very long legs, he moved slowly, as if he had all the time in the world. Louisa could very well imagine him a marionette with an unskilled puppeteer pulling at his strings.

"What have you got there?" Ox asked.

Quiet Si held a hammer in one hand and in the other a large wooden board attached to a long wooden stake. Louisa tipped her head to better read the words slanted across it.

Closed Due to Misfortunate Circumstances

"Oh, the carnival can't close," Jess said. "The mess isn't so bad—"

A loud boom sounded from one of the nearest tents. Everyone turned, watching as the structure wobbled and swayed, and then folded in on itself. Louisa flinched as dust and leaves clouded the air where it had fallen.

"Well." Jess pouted, proven quite wrong.

"But the carnival has never closed before," Mercy said. "Has it?" She looked to Quiet Si, who had been there longer than any of them.

"Oh," he said. "It has. It was."

He continued past them, lowering the sign, as if it had grown heavy. The stake dragged through the dirt. Mercy, Ox, and Jess raced after him, crowding close and tossing out questions, each one louder than the one before.

"When did it close?"

"For how long?"

"What happened?"

Not wanting to miss his answer, Louisa caught up to them, leaning in just as Quiet Si said, "It was all so long ago. When the stars were almost in reach."

He might have said more, but in Louisa's bag, the love bugs started clicking. It was most distracting, and curious too, for she had not been feeling overly sad just then but rather grateful for her rescue. She unfastened the buttons, hoping the little pests would leave her for good.

Quiet Si turned at her shuffling. His strange wooden-eyed gaze fell on Louisa, and he tilted his head, all the better to see her with his one good eye. "I thought you had flown free."

"I could not get past the storm," Louisa said.

His jaw groaned, wood against bone, as he worked it

side to side. "It's waiting and watching." It was a peculiar thing to say, but Quiet Si was a peculiar sort of person, Louisa supposed. Still, it sent a shiver through her body—that he too might have felt the tremble of dark magic.

"You didn't finish telling us about the last time the carnival closed," Mercy said. "When was it?"

"It was the day I arrived." Quiet Si gripped the hammer. His wooden knuckles creaked. "The day all the stars fell."

Ox scratched his head. "Oh, sure. Right."

Mercy elbowed him.

"I slept for a very long time. So long I lost sight of all my yesterdays along with my name." Quiet Si stared off into the middle distance, caught somewhere in the past. Louisa could not guess what he might be thinking, or what memories he might be trying to recall.

Jess plastered a funny smile on her face and said much too cheerfully, "Let's find Fiona and Darcelle. They'll want to know we're okay."

Louisa nodded, watching Quiet Si a moment longer. He lugged the sign forward, heaving it over a section of the fence that had fallen, and then pierced the ground with its sharp stake. The pounding of his hammer echoed behind them as they walked away.

"Well, the day all the stars fell, I think a big one must've hit his head," Jess said.

"*Hard*," Ox agreed.

Mercy, Ox, and Jess hopped over a log in the center of the path, and Louisa floated right over it.

"I feel sorry for him. His memories seem awfully muddled," she said. "What did he mean he lost his yesterdays and his name?"

"We all have. I mean, everyone knows me as Merciless the Spider, not Mercedes Valencia, which is my *real* name."

"I am Jessamine Martel." A smile spread on Jess's face and she giggled. "Did you really think Ox had no other name?"

Louisa might have thought Ox a strange name, but she would not have told him so. "What is it, then?" she asked.

"Uh-uh, no, I'm not telling." He shook his head. His cheeks turned pink. "I go by Ox now."

"Your real name must be truly awful if you prefer Ox," Mercy teased.

He did not deny it and quickly changed the subject, swinging his face toward Louisa. "Are you going to stay?"

She took one last look at the cloud-darkened sky, at the way it waited and watched. "For now, at least."

But she also remembered what Ox had told her—that no one who had been invited to stay at the carnival had ever left it.

↶ 16 ↷
A DIFFERENT KIND OF GRAVITY

The next morning, Louisa set to work mending her coat. She'd sewn nothing for weeks and weeks, and now, as she set a slow but careful pace and the black thread wove in and out, she could almost feel the gentle hand of her mother guiding her needle.

And she heard the soft words the seamstress had spoken the night before as well, when Louisa and the others had gone to her tent.

I could use another set of hands such as yours, skilled with a needle and thread. Poor Darcelle had fainted during the storm, leaving her face the palest white, her hair lackluster around her shoulders, and her temple marred with the smallest bruise. Equally distressing, her once-beautiful chandelier now hung like a skeleton, its silver bones intact but all its crystals fallen and shattered.

Understandably, she wasn't up to the task of mending the tents, but Louisa was more than eager to be of use. Just as soon as she sewed up her coat.

Louisa pulled it closer, placing the sleeve at a better angle. Something clinked and fell out of the pocket. She stabbed the needle into the sleeve so she would not lose it and then reached to the ground.

The copper coin glinted in the sunlight as she plucked it up. She turned it this way and that, the whisper of a thought tickling at the back of her mind.

It was not the misfortune itself she was trying to think of just then. To be sure, Fiona's words had swamped her with doubt. But it was something else Fiona had said. Something about a coin.

And then the words came to her.

But remember, like a coin, there are two sides to this misfortune. Will you consider what I could not see? What only you can see? What your heart tells you?

Louisa pushed the coin back into her pocket and continued her mending but with much less attention and care. She tugged against an overlarge stitch, and the thread snapped.

If each misfortune has two faces, of which Fiona can see but one, I only have to turn over the coin and peek at the other side. Yet, try as she might, she could not see the other side of her misfortune clearly. Her mind spun with the idea that she would one day know her father—that's what she felt in her heart.

Louisa bowed her head, pressing white knuckles to her eyes to push back the threat of tears. (Though the love bugs thirsted for them, not a single one fell.)

With a great sigh, she rethreaded the needle, fixing her sloppy work as best she could. Unfortunately, there would be no hiding the jagged stitches. They stood out on her coat the same way Louisa had stood out in Plum Square when the vendors had glanced down at her feet and seen the untouched ash beneath them.

Needle in hand, Louisa froze. All her life she'd hidden instead of allowing herself to stand out. She'd covered the space between her boots and the ground, working so hard to go unnoticed. But that did not mean she had to. She might float into the air for anyone to see.

For her father to see.

If her misfortune foretold that she would not find him, maybe the other side of the coin showed that *he* would find *her*.

If she left stepping-stones, so he knew where to come . . .

A shadow fell across the ground, intruding on her thoughts. She shivered, not liking the odd shape of the shadow or the way it moved so quickly toward her. All at once it expanded, and, like a monster escaped from under the bed, Mercy sprang forward. "Louisa!"

Louisa jumped to her feet, heart thundering. "You scared me." Mercy grinned as if that was just what she had intended. Louisa's cheeks warmed, hoping Mercy could not tell that thoughts about her father were running wild through her head. She pulled on her coat, tucking the shiny idea away. It felt much too soon to tell anyone just yet. "What is it? Is Jess back from the market?"

"No, she's still with Fiona in Plum. Come look. They're raising another tent."

They ran down the path to where a crowd had formed. Ox stood before the fallen beams of wood and the collapsed tarps. He did not use pulleys and rope, or scaffolding and ladders, but rather the magic within him.

The tent swirled skyward, turning an unnecessary but delightful circle in the air. Louisa and Mercy tipped back their heads, dizzy under the stripes spinning black and gold. One by one the beams groaned upright, and the tent settled into place.

Ox swung around, wiping sweat from his brow as he did so. Though his face was pale from his efforts, he grinned at Louisa and Mercy.

"How does it look?" Ox probably thought Louisa smiled at his magic. And she did, but not the kind he imagined. Friendship was a sort of magic all its own and one she'd had little experience with until recently.

Louisa felt suddenly shy. "It's amazing." Hoping to hide her blushing, she slipped past him, breathing in sharply and lifting into the air. She moved toward the tent, ready to mend the tears.

"You're getting better at that," Ox called.

The compliment sent Louisa floating even higher.

◁ ★ ▷

Each day, Louisa worked alongside the others (or rather, she worked *above* them, practicing her floating as she stitched the tents), returning the carnival to its former splendor. And each night, she watched the performers practice their acts, preparing for the carnival's reopening. There was not a spare second to be found, and only belatedly did Louisa realize the strange storm had passed on, the autumn sky was clear, and yet still she remained at the carnival.

She'd thought long and hard about her idea—that her father might be the one to find her—but she did not know how to go about sharing this plan, fearful everyone would think her foolish. After all, her mother had waited and waited, and Louisa's father had not come.

She could not sit back and wait. Somehow, she would have to lure him to her.

"I think I ought to stay another day," she told Fiona, and Fiona squeezed her shoulder tight and said, "Stay as long as you like. Your skills have not gone unnoticed."

"I think I ought to stay until Darcelle feels better," she told Quiet Si a day later, and he looked to the stars and said, "She said that you would."

"I think I ought to stay until the carnival reopens," she

told Ox, Mercy, and Jess the next evening, and their eyes lit up and Ox said, "Well, of course," as if he and the others had known Louisa's plan all along.

But not the whole of it.

"You might have your own show," Mercy said, and then, instead of lowering her voice, she added quite loudly, "I bet you would outperform Wingless Raven on her night-rope. Imagine if you took her place and became Wingless Louisa."

A group of performers passed by, casting sidelong looks at Mercy's outburst.

"Hush," Jess scolded, smothering a giggle. "They'll think you don't like Raven."

"They can think what they want." Mercy laughed. "I can't help it if Louisa could offer a show even more astounding. Come on, I'll show you."

Louisa knew Mercy didn't mean it and that she only hoped to convince Louisa to stay, just as Ox had.

They hurried past the big top, which was still missing its roof, and piled into the tent just beside it. Rows of benches circled the interior, and they tumbled into the very last row. Fire-Red Rosalyn and some of her friends were gathered on a bench across the tent from them and Annalyse (the rider of the pale mare) and other marvels and mystiques took up the front rows. Quiet Si stood in a corner all alone, while Fiona sat beside Darcelle, who had risen from her bed for the very first time since the storm.

None of them noticed Louisa and the others entering the tent. All their eyes faced upward.

That is, all except Darcelle's, Louisa noticed. The seamstress bowed her head—though her tall stack of hair must have been heavy—and focused on the golden leotard in her lap and the needle and thread in her hands.

When the music began—a low violin played by a marveled hand—Louisa tore her gaze away, looking up.

Wingless Raven perched on the night-rope strung high above. Louisa herself never worried about falling, yet she gulped nervously as Raven stepped from the platform to the rope. There was no netting below.

Although Raven took careful steps, she wobbled, a startled expression on her face. Louisa knew that building tension was all part of the act, but it did not stop her from being swept up in the excitement and danger. Even Fiona gasped, and she must have seen Raven perform countless times before.

When Raven reached the opposite end, she flipped head over heels, hands catching the rope, and then sprang upward. She landed perfectly, bare feet setting down one in front of the other, her arms spread wide.

Louisa clasped her hands together so she would not use them to cover her eyes.

The violin's tune sped faster, and keeping in sync with its rhythm, Raven cartwheeled her way down the rope. At the end, she curtseyed, and the music went silent.

But Raven was far from done with her act. She went forward quite simply, one small step at a time. The bow teased a single, long note from the violin. Raven leaped into splits. On the descent, her front leg bent gracefully, and she caught herself on the rope by the crook of one knee. Her back arched, her arms swept wide, and dangling upside down, she lifted her head, grinning at the audience.

"How does she do it?" Louisa whispered. No matter what Mercy had said, Louisa would never match Raven's grace.

Jess leaned over and cupped her hand to Louisa's ear. "Magic."

It was the truest (and least helpful) answer Jess could have given. All Louisa could think was that Raven must have had a different kind of gravity, a sticky sort that held her to anything she touched.

Raven twirled herself back up to standing. She took one step and then another. Again, she wobbled side to side.

This time Louisa did not even flinch.

But Raven did. She swatted her hand through the air, batting away something Louisa could barely see.

Something as insubstantial as a *shadow*.

Raven's feet slipped out from under her.

She did not catch herself by the knee.

She did not grab hold of the rope with her hand.

Instead, Wingless Raven fell.

⊱ 17 ⊰
SOMETHING SO LOVELY

Someone shrieked. The bow scratched a horrible note across the violin.

Louisa watched in horror as Raven plummeted toward the ground.

The tent went dark, swarmed with shadows from all sides. They flew through the air like smoke and lightning.

Like the threads of the storm that had chased Louisa.

She inhaled so quickly she floated a foot above the bench. A scream stuck at the back of her throat. Mercy jumped to her feet, and Jess buried her face in the folds of Mercy's skirt.

Through the shadows, Raven tumbled. She landed in a crumpled heap, but the impact was almost gentle.

"Was I quick enough?" Ox's golden eyes shone through the darkness, wide and startled as he looked up at Louisa.

Jess peeked out from behind the skirts.

Louisa's heart thudded; her hands shook. Too overcome to speak. She stared in amazement, awed by Ox's magic.

Quiet Si was the first to reach Raven, moving more swiftly than Louisa had ever seen before. He knelt by Raven's side, so careful as he inspected her injuries. Everyone rose from their seats and either rushed to help or covered their mouths in shock.

Jess clutched Louisa's hand, tugging her lower in the air. "She's all right, isn't she?"

Fiona strode toward them, her hair sprouting flowers uncontrolled. Violets and bluebells and teacup roses bloomed and then drifted to the ground. They formed a delicate path behind her. She seemed not to notice as she swept in front of Louisa and the others, standing so her skirts, colored ginger, emerald, and white, blocked their view of Raven's limp form. "You should not see this." She ushered them toward the tent's entrance.

Without argument, Jess went first, turning her head away, and then Mercy and Ox walked forward in a daze. As for Louisa, she cast a backward glance, resisting Fiona's pressure on her shoulder just long enough to see Raven put a hand to her head and whisper, "What happened?" and to hear someone reply, "It was the shadows! They pushed you!"

Louisa stopped dead, unmoving until Fiona nudged her out into the night. "Everything will be fine," Fiona said dismissively. A pansy uncurled on a strand of her hair. "Off you go. I will bring news later." Before Louisa could say a word, Fiona swept closed the curtain.

So many questions tumbled through Louisa's head. If the same thing that had come after her in the woods had gone after Raven just now.

But it couldn't have, could it? The carnival was supposed to be safe. Louisa felt rather unsteady on her ungrounded feet.

"Ox, you saved her!" Jess exclaimed, and Louisa hurried over to their sides.

"I did, didn't I?" Ox wore a look of astonishment, eyes as wide as the moon above. His cheeks flushed despite the chill of the autumn air.

"You were amazing," Louisa said, wanting only to think about Ox saving Raven.

But she could not get those words out of her head, spoken like an accusation. *It was the shadows!* If they blamed the shadows for Raven's fall, they must have blamed their spinner as well.

They must have blamed Mercy.

Yes, Louisa had seen Raven swat at something in the air, like the thin thread of a shadow, but she knew Mercy couldn't have had anything to do with it. Mercy couldn't have meant it when she teased about Louisa taking over Raven's show. She couldn't have sent the shadows. It was only some unfortunate accident.

Or was it a misfortunate accident? At one point during the performance, Fiona had gasped. Louisa could not help but wonder if Fiona had foreseen what would happen.

And if, like the threads of darkness in the woods, it wasn't actually an accident at all.

◁ ★ ▷

Days later, the carnival still hummed with talk of Raven's fall. No one could quite believe that someone so skilled on the rope, and with magic that stickied her to anything, could suffer a spill so tragic. It could have ended much worse, of course, but with a broken leg and a knot on her head, Raven would not soon be returning to her act.

She'd also found a sudden streak of silver in her dark hair, and Louisa was not the only one to think it a strange occurrence.

Raven seemed to have no better an understanding of what had happened. "It was like something cut sharply into my magic," she had explained, fingers running through her newly silvered strand of hair. She'd kept a watchful eye on Mercy, as if someone had told her what Mercy had said— that Louisa would take her act and her name.

Louisa said nothing of what she'd heard that night about what might be to blame. *It was the shadows!* And if Mercy noticed the sidelong looks angled her way and the whispers that echoed her name, she also said nothing.

Hoping to push such thoughts from her head, Louisa tried

to concentrate on the task before her—untangling a rather stubborn length of thread so she could mend another section of tent—but she caught sight of Darcelle Duval coming straight toward her and somehow managed to worsen the knotting.

"I've been looking for you everywhere," Darcelle said, her voice thin.

It must only have been that Darcelle wasn't fully recovered from her fainting spell, and it fatigued her to be up and about, Louisa reasoned. But she did not look overtired. Her long red skirt matched the red of her lips, and her hair was plaited and piled on top of her head, a vibrant red once again without a strand out of place.

"Do you need something of me?" Louisa asked.

"Yes. I could use your hand with the costumes."

Louisa loved her work with the tents. Closing huge tears and making them whole again. It made her feel a part of the carnival. But more delicate stitching reminded Louisa of her mother. The two of them sitting side by side, quiet more often than not but for the running of threads through fabric, the snapping of the fire in the hearth, and the humming of her mother happy (and not) beside her.

But another part of Louisa fluttered with nerves. She was used to old garments of clothing that needed mending to last another winter or dresses begging for lengthening when a girl grew taller. The carnival's costumes were another matter.

Darcelle turned back down the path. "Come."

Louisa followed the seamstress to her tent. The chandelier still hung from its ceiling. Louisa had thought none of the red crystals remained, but a few of them clinked against one another, bright and sparkly and good as new. Costumes were laid out across every surface.

"I have been hard at work ensuring everything is ready for the reopening."

"There seems little you would need me to do," Louisa remarked. Maybe Darcelle only wanted her to go over the costumes one last time, making sure no buttons were missing and no loose threads poked from the seams.

Darcelle plucked up a golden leotard, so sparkling and bright with sequins it put the stars in the sky to shame. Glitter dusted the sheer sleeves, and the short skirt flared from the waist, striped black and gold. It looked like the very leotard Darcelle had been sewing the night Raven fell from the nightrope.

"Isn't it nice?" Darcelle fussed with the elaborate collar, as if she knew it was perfect but was much too modest to boast.

"It's magnificent," said Louisa. In fact, she had never seen anything she liked so much, not even her favorite dress, which her mother had sewn with love.

"It's for you." The corners of Darcelle's mouth lifted.

Louisa took a step back, feeling much the same as she had the first time she'd entered the seamstress's tent—that everything was too beautiful to touch. "For me?"

"Of course. Though as I took no measurements, you must try it on to be certain it fits."

Tempted, Louisa reached out. She ran one finger along the black ribbon around the waist of the skirt. Most decidedly satin. "But why? When would I ever wear it?"

"Can't you guess?" Darcelle laughed. "We need you." There was a desperate note to her words. "Poor Raven cannot perform. But you can."

Louisa traced her finger along the sleeve of the leotard, the material so thin she hardly felt it. Against the skin of her arms, it would feel only like air.

She shook her head, snapping out of her reverie. She did not want to cast more suspicion upon Mercy by stepping into this role. Besides, Raven would heal. She would once again walk the night-rope, defying gravity and charming the crowd below.

And Louisa knew so little of her magic. Only the trouble it got her into. She could not manage or control it. Even the wind could command her more surely. Ox might have thought that her skill had improved, but after lifting in the air, she could not even find a way down on her own no matter how often she practiced.

"I am terrible with magic!" It came out in a rush, and with it, the desire—so strong, so new—to be better. Everyone around her brimmed with magic and knew how to wield it.

But Louisa, she was like a feather. Swept here to there. Unable to save her mother. Unable to find her father. What good was one feather alone when wings were needed for flight?

"My dear, my dear," said Darcelle. "You are untaught, unlearned, but not unskilled."

"Do you really think so?"

"Oh, but I know it."

Hesitantly, Louisa accepted the costume, wanting so much to believe Darcelle's words. She slipped behind a narrow changing screen and traded her coat and dress for the golden leotard with the striped skirt. It fit her better than anything she owned.

"Let me see," Darcelle said, and Louisa stepped out into the open.

She did not feel like herself, and when she caught a glimpse of her reflection in the mirror, she realized she did not look like herself either. Instead, she looked like someone who would be noticed, someone who would take to the sky, confident and sure in the air. Someone who might draw crowds that would spread word of her act far and wide until it reached the ears of her father.

And he would come for her!

Darcelle looked her over from head to toe. She did not ask again if Louisa would stay. It must have been written on her face, the smallest, most hopeful smile slipping out.

"You have much to practice and little time. Everything must be perfectly magical," Darcelle said. "The carnival gates will open in three nights."

↳ 18 ↲
WINDSWEPT

Louisa floated in the center of the tent, unable to move any higher and unable to lower herself to the ground. She had been practicing for two days and had little to show for it. Rather quickly she could find her way into the air, upward of ten feet, which seemed a great height, out of reach of grasping hands, even of Quiet Si, who was so very tall. She could also spin a circle or two. But that was all.

Standing in the dirt below, Ox, Mercy, and Jess looked up at her, hands on their hips and unimpressed frowns on their faces. Louisa could not read Quiet Si's wooden expression, but he stood there as well, apart from the others, very still and very thoughtful.

"Do *something*," Mercy said, which was not at all helpful. "You will bore the crowds if you only hover there."

"I am trying," Louisa said.

"Not like that." Again, Mercy was firm with a correction, and Louisa had no idea why Mercy had ever thought she could be more astounding than Wingless Raven.

Louisa swept her arms through the air with the hope it would move her forward.

"You look like you're swimming. Do you want to be known as *Floundering Lou: Fish of the Air*?" Mercy might have intended to draw a stern voice, for it dipped low and scratchy, but she smiled as she said it. Ox snorted, and Jess fell into a fit of laughter.

Louisa could not think of a worse name. "I want only to be known as Louisa LaRoche."

"But you have to have one." Jess squinted her eyes at Louisa, as if for inspiration.

"For now I'm just hoping I can improve enough to perform at all," Louisa said. Her act would draw her father to the carnival. The first stepping-stone tossed out to him. She lowered her arms and focused on her feet, but they didn't seem to want to do anything other than dangle there.

"I know what you need, Louisa LaRoche," Jess teased. She held her hands against each cheek and let out a breath, the way she might blow the seeds from a dandelion.

"What are you doing?" Ox asked. "Now you're the one who looks like a fish."

"I am imitating the wind," Jess said, as if it were the

most obvious thing in the world, and continued to puff out her cheeks until she turned red in the face.

Quiet Si jolted, body twitching like a marionette. "The wind."

Louisa could not tell if he thought the idea good or bad, but something sparked in her mind. A small bit of worry, yes, for the last wind she'd encountered had nearly sucked her into the sky, but she also remembered it lifting her carefully over the fence at the carnival. Until she better mastered her magic, maybe she could somehow use the wind.

"Ox, help me down!" He lowered her so easily. She drifted to the ground like a leaf.

"You can't give up already," Mercy said.

"I'm not. I wouldn't." This was much too important to her, though she hadn't told them the whole of it.

A twinge of guilt climbed up Louisa's spine. Her motives felt more selfish than selfless. She cared about the carnival and all the people within it—Jess, Mercy, and Ox most of all—but the choice to stay she'd made for herself alone, decided even before Darcelle Duval handed her the leotard. Everything she did was with the purpose of reuniting with her father.

"What have you got in mind?" Ox said.

"I don't know exactly, only this tent is much too stuffy. I think Jess is right."

"I told you." Jess cast a triumphant look at Ox, but then her eyebrows drew together. "What am I right about?"

"I think I need the wind." It constantly tested her. Maybe she needed to accept the challenge.

Quiet Si's wooden eye rolled in his head. Louisa worried he might object, thinking the wind would snatch her away, but when he said nothing, she led them all outside.

The sun sat at the horizon, orange rays of light spreading above them. She had not thought it so late. Already, the stars glowed dimly.

"The stars," Louisa whispered.

"What about them?" Ox looked up at them and then away. They appeared no different than usual, of course.

"I have an idea!" Louisa started running. She was too excited to explain it all. Instead, she would show them.

"Wait up!" Jess tore after her, as did Ox and Mercy.

Quiet Si followed too. Louisa could hear the heaviness of his footsteps.

Down the pathway Louisa went until she reached the big top. It was still missing its roof, and little repair had been done to it. It stood there abandoned and waiting.

And windswept.

The slightest breeze gusted. Wind chimes rang in the near-night, softer than usual.

Jess, Ox, and Mercy gathered around her. Quiet Si slipped ahead of them into the tent.

"Fiona said it's coming down tomorrow since there isn't enough time to fix the roof," Mercy said.

"Why does it need one?" Louisa asked. "This is the Carnival Beneath the Stars, is it not?"

"Oh!" Jess clapped her hands together. "Do you mean to perform here? It's too perfect."

"I wish I had thought of it," Ox said with a grin.

Louisa looked to Mercy, hoping for her approval as well and knowing it would be the hardest to earn. "Boring?"

"Not boring," Mercy declared.

Even more hopeful now, Louisa was about to duck into the tent, when Jess said (for at least the hundredth time), "I am so happy you decided to stay."

"Me too," Ox said. "But what about finding your father? Have you given up on him?" Ox looked so worried, so hurt, probably thinking of his own father and wishing he stood at his side. Yet just like Louisa's mother, there was no getting him back from the beyond.

Jess's and Mercy's faces grew long and serious, as if they too had suffered great loss. Maybe they wouldn't think Louisa's hopes foolish and selfish. Maybe they wrestled the love bugs and would understand.

"Have you lost someone too?" she asked them.

Mercy tipped her face away and buttoned her lips, as if it hurt too much to speak of. There was so much she didn't say—about her past, about everyone whispering of the shadows that caused Raven's fall. Mercy kept her secrets close.

Jess's eyes went round. "I miss my sisters."

"I'm sorry," Louisa said, struck with another pang of guilt that she had not thought to ask before.

"Oh, they're okay," Jess said, swinging her voice high and merry, though it rang with a false note. "My parents turned me out last year. Too many of us underfoot, and I'm the oldest. Nearly thirteen. I can take care of myself."

"Of course you can," Mercy said.

Louisa had not meant to turn a happy moment sad. She smiled and echoed Mercy's words. "You can." No wonder Jess smothered them in hugs and clung to their hands. She had already been separated from her sisters and must have worried anyone she cared for might slip from her grasp just as they had.

"And your father?" Ox asked again.

Louisa should have told them all along, and so she pushed on. "Fiona gave me my misfortune. She said I will never find my father. But I haven't given up on him."

"Oh no," Jess said.

"I am trying to understand the unseen side of my misfortune, the part hidden to Fiona. I . . . I hope, if I am good enough, if I master my mystique, my father will hear of my performance and that *he* will find *me*." She felt so vulnerable saying it all aloud, so the words came in a rush.

"He is sure to come," Ox said.

"Do you really think so?" Relief ran through her that she'd told them the whole of it and that they thought her plan might work.

"We'll make flyers and send them around," Jess said.

"We'll put an advertisement in the newspaper," Ox added, as if they too wanted to leave stepping-stones for her father.

"He'll come," Mercy said. "Only if you are not boring." A playful challenge lit her eyes.

It was just the motivation Louisa needed. "Tomorrow night, maybe I will have a longer line outside my tent than yours."

Mercy grinned. "We'll see about that."

They scrambled into the tent, Louisa more eager than any of them. Quiet Si must have heard them, as they made a great deal of noise, but he stood rooted to the ground and his gaze never wandered from the sky. Above the roofless tent, stars blinked and twinkled. Louisa could not imagine a better stage. No eye in the crowd would be able to look away from the view. Or from her, she hoped.

The wind swept lazily through the tent. Louisa let it hold her, let it lift her, let it spin her in a dizzy circle.

For a moment, she felt so sure, like she was meant to fly, but when she glanced down, she thought of Raven tumbling from the night-rope to the ground. And when she glanced up, she thought of becoming lost in the forest of stars. She froze, not because she feared falling or floating away, but because she feared failing.

"It's okay." Quiet Si spoke at last, his voice reassuring and soft. "Magic is tricky, but so are you."

From somewhere below, Jess giggled.

Louisa hovered in place. She felt stuck and helpless and not at all tricky. "How so?"

"You know best. You know your *magic* best. It hums inside every part of you." He spoke as if he knew the feeling, sensitive to those vibrations. "Take a step."

He asked for such a small thing, but it seemed impossible. She was so high in the air and didn't know how to navigate. "I can't," she said.

"Close your eyes."

Although she did not think it would help, Louisa shut her eyes. The breeze swept through her hair. It nudged her the same as Quiet Si.

"Think of it as a game, and take just one step." When he was not swamped with distraction, his voice carried strong and true, an encouraging offstage whisper reminding a performer of their act.

Below, she heard his wooden joints shifting and the heavy placement of his boots as he set them down. Determined, Louisa pushed her heel off from the air, taking one step and then another, in rhythm with Quiet Si.

Louisa's heart swelled. Her careful steps were much the same as when she'd followed in her mother's soot-prints. A game of sorts, a *trick* of sorts. But when it came time to perform, she would not be chasing after her mother, and Quiet Si would not be walking beneath her. She'd be alone with the stars.

Her eyelids fluttered open. She gazed at the night and the stardust tumbling all around her. It shone and sparkled, like golden soot. Louisa could make her own marks here, up in the sky no one else touched. If only she were brave enough to let her magic loose.

In and out she breathed, letting her excitement mount. Tingles warmed her belly. Maybe it was the magic humming within her, as Quiet Si had said.

Louisa sprang forward, hopping through the glimmering light in just the manner she'd chased her mother through the sooty streets of Plum.

Ox, Jess, and Mercy cheered her on.

Louisa leaped faster. She skipped. She ran.

The movement felt no different all these feet in the air than it did inches off the ground. Except this time she was not trying to hide her magic. Her *gift*.

She swirled back to the center of the tent. Beaming, she dipped into a curtsy. "I did it!"

"Now you will learn to soar," said Quiet Si, and Louisa no longer thought it impossible.

⸌ 19 ⸍
THE STARLARK

Louisa did not sleep that night. While her friends crafted the loveliest of flyers to send out into the world, she worked on a project of her own—sewing a kite with the lightest of Darcelle's golden fabric.

A photograph of her father rested beside her as she worked, the one with the kite trailing behind him. Louisa designed her kite exactly the same as his—the diamond-shaped body, the thin crisscrossing lengths of wood for its frame, and the long, long tail made of dazzling ribbons and bows. Flying high, it would be eye-catching. Wherever he was, maybe he would see it, recognize it, stepping onto this stone she'd leave for him.

Once she completed it, she spent the rest of the night practicing (even after everyone else, red-eyed and yawning, crawled off to bed). She needed to rehearse, of course, but also, she hoped to avoid anyone other than her friends. The other performers' whispers about Raven's fall had grown less whispery and all the more suspicious of Mercy. It did not help how Mercy told everyone about Louisa's mystique. How she always insisted Louisa's act rivaled Raven's.

As if they thought Mercy might have interfered with Raven's performance so that Louisa could have a place at the carnival.

Pushing such thoughts from her mind the next day too, she rehearsed over and over with only the briefest of naps right there in the tent, until she had mastered each step, each turn, each gesture as best she could—chasing the soot of stars.

When she finally stepped out of the tent that evening, the carnival shone bright beneath the dark sky. The black-and-gold tents stood tall and grand, the gilded carts overflowed with trinkets and baubles, food and drink, and soon the line at the ticket booth would run through the Spark Woods all the way to the road.

Louisa slipped away from the last-minute preparations, darting along the pathway toward the back section of the carnival, which housed the living quarters. Maybe she should have been tired, but she overflowed with excitement.

When she entered the small tent that she'd come to share with Mercy and Jess, they were in the middle of painting each other's faces. Mercy dusted bronze sparkles onto Jess's cheeks, and Jess ran a black-tipped stick over Mercy's lips. In the soft glow of the fiery lights overhead, they looked magical, one dressed entirely in black with her dark hair twisted up in silver clips, the other with shiny blond hair wearing the brightest gold. They turned to her with their half-done faces, both lovely and strange at once.

"You're back at last! We thought we'd have to drag you away from the tent," Jess said. "You are just in time to get ready. Quick, quick, put on your costume."

It hung from a low beam, as brilliant as Louisa remembered it. Maybe even more so, as she could now envision herself wearing it up in the air, twirling and twirling until the skirt spun around her.

Except something about it seemed different. At first, she could not say what, but then she realized there was a flash of color that hadn't been there before. Two red slashes fell between the folds of the skirt. She touched the stripes, losing her hand in the material. "It's got pockets!"

"Oh yes." Mercy held up the brush in her hand and said to Jess, "Close your eyes." And then to Louisa, she said, "Quiet Si asked Darcelle to sew them in. He told her he had another idea for your show. So, you'd better hurry up and find out what he means."

"I wonder what it could be." Louisa began changing, ripping off her coat and dress behind the low changing screen, and then carefully pulled on the leotard. "My head is already stuffed full of choreography. I don't think I will be able to remember anything else." Louisa straightened her skirt, admiring the red pockets, and rejoined Mercy and Jess.

"Your turn." Mercy's darkened eyes, in their masklike glitter, looked at Louisa mischievously.

"I've never been made up before."

Jess glanced down at the pallet of powders and shadows, as if they were as marvelous as the beads and other trinkets she sold at her cart each night, and picked up a small pot filled with glitter. "It will be fun."

Louisa sat down on the little chair they pointed her to, and as they poked their sparkling brushes into her face and fussed with her long, long hair, she thought it might be more fun for them than for her. But she sat patiently and quietly, without complaint, even when the powder tickled her nose and Jess's brush jabbed her in the eye. Even when Mercy plucked a pin from her own knotted strands and swept up a section of Louisa's locks, stabbing the point against her scalp.

When they were through, Jess handed Louisa a small hand mirror. "Have a look-see."

Louisa peeked at her reflection, smiled her red lips, and fluttered her gold-touched eyelids. She looked very much like her mother, which made her heart first cinch, then swell. She struggled to keep it locked tight.

Louisa set down the mirror, glass to the table, as if it

might still hold her reflection even after she'd turned her face away. She smiled, but only briefly, for so much weighed on her mind. "I'd better go find Quiet Si," she said, pulling her coat on over her costume. "I'll see you later."

With the kite she'd made in hand, she slipped from the tent and set about finding Quiet Si. With one ear tilted, she listened for the weighted sound of his boots, and after some wandering, she spotted him ahead on the pathway.

She caught up to him easily at the carnival's entrance. She stood beside him as he removed the *Closed Due to Misfortunate Circumstances* sign and kicked dirt into the hole left by the stake.

"How are the stars tonight?" she asked in greeting, having found that while he did not talk often, he did love speaking of the stars. She hoped they dominated the sky, as clouds would ruin her show.

"They are fine. And she is the brightest." He gazed up.

"She?" Louisa wondered if he had lost the way of his story even before it had begun. She could not always follow his train of thought. Sometimes he seemed unable to keep track of all the threads in his mind, plucking different ideas from the murky corners of his brain and placing them together, unaware one had little to do with the other.

But he did not say more.

At last, he glanced back at Louisa. "You have a star catcher."

"It's just a kite," she said, but really, it was so much more. She might not have been trying to catch a star, but she *was* hoping to catch her father. "Will you help me raise it?"

Quiet Si took it from her hands and tossed it skyward. The wind swept it up and up and up. Louisa clutched the silver thread, knotting it around the beam of the fence. The kite bobbed in the air, tail streaming.

Crickets chirped in the night, filling the quiet between them—as did the love bugs. Louisa had been thinking of nothing but the lovely kite and the stars and her performance, her sadness for once far removed, so she did not know why the love bugs hounded her.

Quiet Si heaved the sign over his shoulder and turned back to the carnival. A long-haired boy with a black velvet coat had already taken his place in the ticket booth, awaiting the first arrivals. The sound of wind chimes tinkled (though Louisa had never seen them strung anywhere around the carnival), and she remembered how she'd heard them as she traveled through the Spark Woods for the very first time.

So much had changed.

"I'm nervous."

Quiet Si paused, looking down at Louisa. Shadows folded into the odd angles of his wooden jaw and cheek, but the strangeness of his face no longer surprised her. It only felt familiar. "You are ready," he said simply.

"But what are the pockets in my skirt for?" she asked.

His face creaked into a slow smile.

◁ ★ ▷

Still as stone, Quiet Si stood in the middle of the hushed tent. His wooden chin rested on his chest; his hands hung at his sides. Every part of him slumped.

A cello played low. A light swooped round. Quiet Si lifted his head, wobbly on his neck before he straightened it, and peered at the audience with his one good eye. The other stared off, unseeing. Gasps trickled through the darkened rows. Louisa watched him as breathlessly as everyone else.

He raised one arm and tipped his crinkled top hat to the crowd four times, facing a different section each time. Welcoming one and all. Each of his movements swung crooked with exaggeration, as if someone unseen tugged at invisible strings. When he spoke, his wooden jaw moved stiffly. All part of the act, Louisa knew, but he seemed more puppet than human.

"Children!" he called, appealing to them first and foremost. "You will soon be squealing in delight. You will be marveling at impossibilities. At the outrageous heights reached. At the idea that someone can touch the stars and sky."

His voice came strong and true, just as it had when he'd

guided her how to use her mystique. As if talking of magic lit a flame inside him, clearing the clouds that fogged his mind.

Louisa trembled in the shadows, awaiting her entrance. For all she had practiced, she did not know if it had been enough. She realized, suddenly and fiercely, that she did not want to disappoint him or Jess, Mercy, and Ox, who sat somewhere in the crowd.

Most of all, she wanted to soar so high and so marvelously that no matter how far away he was, her father would hear tell of her act and come calling.

"Gentleladies, men, fine folk!" Quiet Si's voice, though soft, carried to even the people in the very last rows. "You will be stunned. You will be mystified. You will think you are seeing a trick." He straightened the collar of his black-and-gold-striped jacket. "But what you are seeing is real! What you are seeing"—his voice turned down to a whisper— "is *magic*."

Louisa's belly twisted into knots. She was not being careful as she had promised her mother, but she was being true to herself, and she knew her mother would approve of that.

"Everyone, everyone, set your eyes on the sky . . ." Quiet Si paused. He turned. He swept his arm out to introduce her. She had all but forgotten a stage name, but he had not, and called, "Set your eyes on *Louisa LaRoche: The Starlark*!"

As Quiet Si slipped away, a light fell upon Louisa and followed her from the edge of the tent to its very center. Louisa stood so small and nervous in the space he'd left behind. Her fingertips fluttered over the hem of her skirt. She looked all around, eyes wild, until she caught sight of Ox and Mercy, and Jess waving happily.

The cello soared, and when it did, Louisa sucked in a breath and soared with it.

She shot into the air, as if tethered to a string and pulled up from the rafters. But when everyone in the crowd tipped back their heads, they immediately could see—there were neither rafters nor ropes, only the sky above overflowing with stars.

Louisa twirled among them, golden and bright. Her skirt rippled in the night's cool wind. Up high, it was easy to forget about the crowd and to perform as if her father were watching. Around and around the tent she went, dipping and twisting like a bird released from its cage.

She forced herself higher, chasing the soot of the stars, past the top of the roofless tent and into the night itself. The air was colder, sharper. She looked down, imagining one of the faces gazing up at her was her father's. She reached for the star-crackers in her pockets—made by Fire-Red Rosalyn specially for Louisa at Quiet Si's request—and snapped their strange casing. Her palms warmed but did not burn.

At a distance, the cello sounded so soft, but when it

struck its deepest note, she threw up her hands, sending the star-crackers skyward. The night crackled and boomed as they burst open, sending streams of gold, silver, and red sparkling through the sky.

From below, Louisa heard the crowd roar.

↜20↝
MINA THE MIRROR

The star-crackers shimmered against the dark sky. Louisa had never seen anything so beautiful. She wondered if the gold, silver, and red shower of light could be seen all the way to Plum and beyond. If a man with hair the color of midnight would glance out his window and see Louisa spinning among the stars.

Dizzy, she searched the faces in the crowd below, but so high up, they blurred together. The crowd clapped and cheered, and when the star-crackers fizzled, everyone finally and reluctantly made their way out of the tent and on to the next attraction.

Louisa grew cold. The moon seemed closer than the ground.

She sighed, dipping a little in the sky, but it was all she could manage. For all her practicing, she still hadn't mastered her descent.

A wisp of a shadow blew past Louisa, as if Mercy meant to tug her from the air with it. "Are you ready to come down from there?" Mercy called.

Louisa hesitated, remembering the shadow Raven had swatted away before her fall. But she couldn't doubt her friend like all the others. "I'm ready," she replied.

"I'll help you." Ox strode over, and the shadow curled away. He lowered her, bit by bit, taking her hand when she floated close enough to reach it, as if he were helping her step down from a high stoop. She didn't mind the heaviness of his magic anymore. Although it was strange, it was also comforting.

Jess bumped Ox out of the way and threw her arms around Louisa. "You were fantastic!" she squealed into Louisa's wind-tangled hair, and then pulled back.

"I could not have done it without all of you. Thank you," said Louisa, not quite believing the show was over already.

"Well, of course. We're friends, aren't we?" Jess asked.

Louisa could feel the tiny cracks in her heart where she'd let it expand, just a bit, just enough to let in Ox, Jess, Mercy, and even Quiet Si. She hadn't been mindful enough of keeping it hardened, and then and there, she sealed up all those little fault lines—not to keep her friends out, but to hold them inside.

Without seeming to realize Louisa hadn't responded,

Jess rattled on. "Oh, and you did it. You won! The line for your show was *much* longer than Mercy's."

"I can't help it if some people are scaredy-cats." Mercy grinned. "But see? You drew an even larger crowd than Raven ever had."

"I would not mind if I had only one person in line, so long as it was my father." Louisa did not mean to sound so solemn, but with so little sleep the night before, she felt suddenly tired. And doubtful of her plan.

"He'll come," Ox said. He must have missed his father very much. "One day soon."

"Yes, but tonight we should celebrate," Jess said.

"We have to," Mercy agreed. "You worked so hard."

Louisa would have liked nothing better than to return to their tent and tuck into sleep, but they had spent so much time helping her, she could not tell them no. But first, she had to thank one last person.

As they debated what treats to eat and what shows to watch, Louisa slipped outside. Quiet Si was positioning the rope in front of the tent, barring anyone from entering. Behind him, a newly painted board announced:

Louisa LaRoche: The Starlark

"Did you make it for me? The sign?" The black lettering matched the writing on all the others, sharp and bold.

Quiet Si lifted his head, but the shadows cast by his top

hat masked his face. "Yes." He turned the board around so people would know the show was over, and displayed the painted star on the other side.

"You did a very fine job. Thank you. Thank you for everything." She never would have reached such heights without Quiet Si's instruction. And his patience.

"You were so close to the stars. Soaring among them like a dream I once had. There could not be a better name for you than *The Starlark*."

Louisa's cheeks warmed. She liked it too, and more, she liked that they'd also honored her request to go by her true name. "Was it Mercy who came up with it, or Jess?"

"One or the other." Quiet Si shifted the stand nearest him, and the black rope strung through it swung back and forth.

Although he hadn't really answered her question, she did not press him. She liked the idea of them deciding on it together. "What is your real name?" she asked instead, for just as she was curious about Ox's real name, she wondered about Si's as well.

"Si is my only name," he said. The pupil of his pale eye enlarged in the dark. "But it's not really mine."

"I'm not sure I understand. Whose is it, then?" She might have asked him more, but a small black insect peeked out from beneath the folds of his collar. It darted over his shoulder, gone too fast to be sure, but she could have sworn it was a love bug. Where had it come from? And *who* had it come for? Surely not Louisa, for she was bursting with joy.

"Was that . . . ? Did you see?" She stumbled over the words.

Quiet Si's wooden jaw creaked. Before he could say a word, Ox, Jess, and Mercy burst from the tent, gathering Louisa up in their storm of excitement.

"You're always running off on us," Mercy said.

"Are you ready?" Ox asked.

"Let's go, let's go." Jess bounced on her heels.

"Go on, then," said Quiet Si with a small smile.

At his words, Louisa waved a hasty goodbye, and they swept her away into the passing crowd. All the sounds of the carnival swirled around her, but somewhere in the night, a love bug wandered restless.

◁ ★ ▷

With heaping bags of caramel corn in their laps, Louisa sat side by side by side with Ox, Mercy, and Jess. They had the very best seats in the tent, first row, front and center. No matter how tired Louisa felt, she tingled with excitement, for she had yet to see this performer.

Mina the Mirror: Magician of Magnificence

When she'd asked about the show, no one would tell her a thing. "It's something you must see for yourself," was all Ox would say about it, and then he elbowed Mercy. "And keep your caramel corn in your mouth this time instead of tossing it on the stage."

Mercy chomped a huge handful of the treat, eyes glinting. "Mina pranked me last. It's only fair I play a little trick of my own."

"Shh," Jess hushed them as the lights in the tent dimmed and a single beam focused on the stage.

Ox leaned over, whispering, "Remember, this is real too."

After all she had seen, Louisa would believe in anything.

A mirror sat alone on the low stage until a girl stepped from behind the curtain. She was perhaps five years older than Louisa and wore a plain black dress trimmed with golden thread that glinted when she moved. Her hair hung undone, long brown waves tossed behind her shoulders.

"We are Mina," she said softly, the look and the sound of her quite ordinary even though her words drew murmurs from the crowd. Louisa peered all over the stage but saw no one else the girl might be referring to. "Some call us a magician. Some call us a girl. Why can't we be both?" She walked over to the mirror and reached out one white hand, touching glass.

Or maybe it wasn't glass, Louisa realized, as no reflection appeared on the surface. It was just an empty frame. Mina stood still, bare feet on the ground.

But somehow, she also stepped forward, one body becoming two.

The first remained unmoving, and the second passed slowly through the frame. Where there had been a lone girl now stood two, one on each side of the mirror-that-was-not-a-mirror. They looked into each other's eyes and smiled.

Louisa thought it must be an illusion. But she remembered Ox's words. *This is real too.*

"Hello, Sister," said the first girl.

"Hello, Sister," said the second girl.

One girl lifted her hand, and the other's movements followed her exactly, just as a reflection would. They gestured gracefully—drawing circles in the air, straightening the hem of their skirt—and lulled the crowd with these simple movements. When one of the girls twisted her hair up into a knot, the other did the same. But when she lowered her arms, her hair fell long and loose over her shoulders, whereas the other girl's hair stayed up, pinned neatly at the base of her neck.

"It is a trick of mirrors and light," someone behind Louisa said.

Louisa wondered what the crowd had whispered during her show.

At the same time, the girls reached forward, clasping their hands together. One pulled, the other yanked. They

swayed back and forth, a tug-of-war, until the first stumbled forward through the mirror's frame, falling into the second. When they collided, they combined. A seamless transition, two girls becoming one. Their hair settled half up, half down, as if they'd made some silent compromise in its styling.

The crowd gasped. They must not have trusted their eyes.

"Together, we are Mina."

When Louisa listened closely, she thought she might have heard two overlapping voices, the slightest hum that one voice alone did not have.

"And apart . . ." The girl twirled one way, and her double spun forth from her body in the other direction. They were identical but for the manner of their hair.

Louisa tipped toward Mercy, so curious about this magic, but she froze before she could pose a single question.

A dark thread chased the girls across the stage. Was Mercy pranking the sisters?

They stopped at the same time, facing the audience, and curtsied. The girl on the right straightened. The girl on the left caught sight of the shadow twining around her ankles. She stumbled backward, dancing out of its reach.

The audience tensed, confused by her missteps. Louisa thought of Raven before her fall, but it couldn't be, it *couldn't* be happening again.

The shadow darkened, snaking up the girl's leg. It

wound around her waist and dabbed a silver splotch on her hair.

The girl let out a terrible scream.

This was no prank, and Louisa could not sit there, watching as another nightmare unfolded. She sprang forward, dumping her bag of caramel corn across the floor and floating to the stage. She swatted at the multiplying shadows. They poked sharp as needles when they brushed her skin, harsher than they'd been in the Spark Woods. She flinched away, but she did not back down. Instead, she soared higher, drawing the threads of darkness after her.

Below, she spotted Ox from the corner of her eye. He'd leaped to the stage and must have lifted the sisters with his magic, for they hung in the air like rag dolls as he brought them behind the curtain.

A shadow dodged forward, slipping after them. Recklessly, bravely, Louisa cut in front of it. The cold, cold touch of needle points sent shivers down her spine.

She darted away, and since she still wore her costume, the crowd must have thought it all some strange act. With puzzled expressions, they leaned forward.

"Do something." Louisa heard Jess's thin plea and found her face in the crowd.

Mercy stood beside her, wide-eyed, ignoring the people in the seats behind her who hissed for her to sit down. Even ignoring Jess, who waved her arms wildly, pointing at the chaos on stage. Mercy met Louisa's eyes for one fragile moment, and then she turned abruptly, bolting down the aisle and out of the tent. Jess tore after her.

Louisa did not know what to think. If anyone should have been able to control the shadows, it would have been Mercy. But instead of helping, she'd fled.

With a sinking heart, Louisa completed a few more turns above the stage, searching for the threads of darkness. Only, they had gone, disappearing as quickly as they had arrived.

Disappearing at the same time as Mercy.

Louisa felt that familiar heaviness in her limbs as Ox magicked her down. When she hovered low enough, she flung herself behind the curtain.

Someone in the audience booed. Children whined that the show had ended too soon. Louisa blocked them out.

"Is it gone?" Ox asked.

"I think so," Louisa said, but she flicked a quick look all around, worried it might be creeping up from behind. "What was it?"

Ox shook his head. "I don't know."

"Isn't it obvious?"

Louisa spun toward the sisters. They sat on the floor, rattled but seemingly unharmed. They clasped each other's hands, fingers entwined. Louisa blinked. No, their fingers were not entwined, they were fused. Where there should have been two hands, there was only one.

After seeing them merge completely, maybe the manner in which they held hands should not have surprised Louisa, but she had never imagined a mystique such as this one—identical twins, wholly individual one moment and inseparable the next.

The sisters traded a look, and then one said, "It was the shadows."

"Yes," said the other. "They attacked us, just as they did Raven."

"But they weren't shadows!" Louisa cried. They'd had a different texture, a different *intent*. Hadn't they?

"What were they, then?" The sisters spoke at the same time.

"Something else," Louisa said stubbornly. It was not a good answer, but she had no better.

"*Someone* else," they accused.

The curtains swung to the side, and Louisa jumped. But it was only Fiona Dior, rushing forward with a distressed look upon her face and hair raining flowers. Jess tumbled in right after her.

Fiona went straight to the sisters, kneeling beside them. Her face betrayed no emotion. "Are you hurt? Are you injured? What happened onstage tonight?"

"We cannot fold together. Not completely," one said between sobs.

"We are broken," cried the other. "Someone means to prevent us from using our magic!"

Louisa swallowed hard. They were not unharmed after all. The dark threads were set on destruction, causing some grievous injury to the sisters' magic. A hollow ache settled in Louisa's stomach.

"Where is Mercy?" Ox whispered.

"She was too fast. I couldn't catch her before she caped herself in shadows," Jess said, still sounding a little winded from running. "Thank goodness Fiona was here."

"We have to find Mercy," Louisa said.

Jess turned. "If she doesn't want to be found—" Her words died on her tongue. Her mouth dropped open. She stared at Louisa and exclaimed, "Your hair!"

"What?" Louisa touched her tangled strands. She glanced down.

The very tips of her midnight-black hair gleamed silver.

~ 21 ~
THE MOON RIDE

Louisa did not think about her silver-tipped hair as Fiona—so focused on the sisters—shooed her, Ox, and Jess from the tent and into the night. She did not think about her silver-tipped hair as they searched the carnival for Mercy, and she did not think about her silver-tipped hair even though Ox and Jess kept stealing glances at it.

She tossed the troublesome strands behind her shoulders, pretending they were no different than before—that she was no different. But a strange sensation tingled along her arms where the thread of darkness had touched her, and the hollow ache in her belly remained.

She would not think of that either.

Instead, she walked with Jess and Ox up and down every path, peeking into every attraction and every shadowed corner. They visited all of Mercy's favorite places, but she wasn't begging Annalyse for a turn on the pale mare or snitching a cinnamon stick from the carnival's best baker or waiting in line for a Moon Ride. She hadn't returned to the girls' tent or the one in which she performed.

"Where could Mercy be?" Louisa asked, stepping past a vendor's long line for spiced pear cider.

"If she drew the shadows close enough, she could be walking beside us right now, and we wouldn't even know it." As if to test his theory, Ox thrust out his elbow—perhaps a little too vigorously. When it connected with nothing but air, he stumbled. His cheeks turned rosy.

On Louisa's other side, Jess did the same, but her elbow jabbed into a man striding by. "Sorry!" she said, but he only smiled at her, as if he and the woman beside him were enjoying the carnival so immensely that nothing could bother him. When he had passed, Jess grumbled, "It's so hard to see anything with all the crowds."

It was true. With so many people moving about, Mercy might slip right past and Louisa wouldn't see her. They needed to get away from the crowds. Louisa turned back, craning her neck and looking up.

A basket sailed by overhead, carried by the moon.

It was so lovely, so *impossible*. Louisa still wasn't used to this particular magic and how far it could reach. Ribbons of silver twisting up and up and up, catching the moon.

"Maybe we can spot her from above." Louisa could float

her way skyward, of course, but all of them together might have better luck.

"I should have thought of that," Ox said with a shake of his head.

"Well, good thing we have Louisa, then." Jess grabbed their hands, turned them around, and pulled them toward the front of the line for the Moon Ride despite the protests from those who would have been next. She approached the carnival worker with a bright smile. "Three, please."

Louisa thought they'd immediately be turned away for skipping, but the woman (who wore a tiny veiled hat and had a dimple in one cheek) lifted the rope to let them pass. "Three favors," she said as they slipped by.

"One favor!" Jess called back, bargaining once again. Perhaps she'd gotten into the habit when settling arguments with her sisters. "I'll watch the line for you tomorrow." The woman waved them on.

And with that, the three of them climbed into the waiting basket and swung shut the little door. Far above, the moon hung fat and nearly full, tethered to the basket with those unbelievably and magically long silver threads. With a single tug to the cord, it lifted them into the sky the same way a hot-air balloon might, but without all the fuss of fire and gas.

"Let's have a good look-see," Jess said.

Hands resting on the rim of the wicker basket, Louisa

leaned forward, and Ox and Jess did the same, each peering over a different side.

Below, the carnival carried on as if nothing were amiss. But those threads of darkness were still out there somewhere. Louisa worried about who they might attack next.

And what they might be taking besides the color of someone's hair.

As she looked for Mercy, the wind blew past, whipping forward Louisa's newly silver tips. Her hair no longer matched her father's, not completely. Now the ends were much the same shade as Quiet Si's.

A half-formed idea flickered in her mind. She glanced toward Ox and Jess. "What if Raven wasn't the first one to have her hair marked by those threads of darkness? What if it started with Quiet Si? He's got a whole head of silver hair."

"That's just because he's old," Ox said.

Jess snickered, still scanning the crowd for Mercy.

"I guess you're right." Louisa turned back around, but she kept hold of the thought to examine later. After all, Quiet Si couldn't have been much older than Darcelle or Fiona, and neither of them had hair his color.

For now, Louisa scoured the grounds with a keen eye, looking for shadows that moved where they shouldn't, but soon, all the bustle of the carnival, all the pockets of gloom, seemed overwhelming.

Ox must have been thinking the same thing, as he sighed. "She's too good at hiding."

"Much too good," Jess agreed. "We'll never find her."

"Of course we will," Louisa said, but her voice trembled and her thoughts spiraled.

How could she ever expect to find her father if they had this much trouble finding Mercy?

"What if my father does not want to be found either?" Louisa couldn't keep the words from bubbling forth. They shook too strongly inside her—this fear she'd locked so tightly in her heart that she'd almost forgotten it was there.

Ox and Jess turned, faces stricken. Neither seemed to know what to say, but then Ox swept his hair to the side without touching it and stepped toward Louisa. He glanced at her with his golden eyes that looked more puppy than beast. "Your father wouldn't leave you. Not if he had a way back to you."

Louisa held his words close, wanting to believe them.

"And if he doesn't have a way back, at least you have us," said Jess, and then she exclaimed, "Oh, look, look." She tipped so far over the edge of the basket that she seemed about ready to tumble out of it.

Louisa and Ox hurried to Jess's side, glancing down at where she pointed. From above, the striped tops of the tents looked more or less the same except for their size, but Louisa spotted the one where Mercy performed right away, for its fabric was entirely black.

Where seconds before it had been pitch dark, now the faintest light flickered at the entrance, as if someone had only just slipped inside.

"Do you suppose she's there now? Waiting until she saw us go before returning?" Jess asked as they began lowering in the sky, a signal that the Moon Ride was coming to an end.

"We'll find out," Ox said.

The basket landed with a gentle thump, and they filed out and into the carnival. Louisa, slowed by her still-heavy thoughts, chased Jess and Ox when they took off at a run . . . but halted when Darcelle Duval stepped into their path.

Tonight, her hair stood even taller, like a ruby crown atop her head, and her full-skirted dress—blood-red with gold-stitched leaves—fell around her like a woodland queen's gown. Though she possessed not a speck of magic, every eye in the carnival turned to look at her, as if she'd spun a spell.

(No one would ever call Darcelle a gob, not even Jess.)

Something about Darcelle's expression—the tightness of her mouth, the height of her arched eyebrows—stopped Louisa from approaching. She ducked behind a vendor's cart, straining to listen. The shadow Mercy had given Louisa sat dark in the depths of her pocket, but she crouched well out of sight and resisted using it to conceal herself further.

Darcelle looked from Ox to Jess. "Where is your mischievous friend?"

"Louisa?" Ox swung his head side to side, belatedly realizing Louisa was not standing beside him. "She was just here."

"No," Darcelle said patiently. "Where is Mercedes?"

Jess shrugged, a hugely exaggerated movement that only emphasized that she might be hiding something. "Haven't seen her."

Louisa tiptoed backward. She had to reach Mercy before Darcelle squeezed the truth out of Jess and Ox.

৬ 22 ৶
MERCILESS THE SPIDER

Louisa approached the all-black tent. It hunkered down between two much larger ones, sinister in its crouched positioning. Shadows sat within shadows.

A rope strung between two posts blocked the entrance. Someone had turned the sign, which meant there were no more shows that evening. Instead of Mercy's stage name, the outline of a long-legged spider marked the backside of the board. Louisa wondered if Quiet Si had painted this too.

Louisa moved cautiously toward the curtain. She parted the ink-black material, and with a quick look over her shoulder to ensure no one saw her enter, she darted inside.

The tent was dark, so dark she worried it might be empty after all. She could not even see her outstretched hand. "Mercy?"

There was no reply.

Louisa turned back the way she had come. Or the way she thought she had come. Shadows had swallowed the entrance.

She swept her arm in front of her. No matter which way she went, her fingertips touched only air. She swatted at the shadows. From somewhere within them came a scratching sound. Louisa did not know if she should move toward it or away, so she stood there, undecided and unmoving except for the trembling of her body.

A faint glow seeped through the shadows, a fog that crept forward slowly. If anything, it was more frightful than the complete darkness had been, for the golden haze exposed the most delicate spiderwebs clinging to the air itself. They draped down from the top of the tent, and they spread out across the floor too.

"Mercy!" she cried. Her feet stumbled forward, webs tangling in the path. She'd never felt so clumsy, so scared. Her heart pounded. Her breaths swept her upward, uncontrolled.

From below, something scampered.

From the darkness, a face appeared.

A warm breath touched Louisa's cheeks. She shrieked.

A low, whip-like voice echoed throughout the tent. "It's about time you came to my show." Caught gracefully in the cobweb crouched Merciless the Spider.

Despite her fright, Louisa was so glad to see Mercy and she was in such awe of her surroundings that at first, all she could do was stare. Some fifteen feet in the air, Louisa floated among the shadow webbing, and Mercy crept along it as if she really were a spider.

"You frightened me," Louisa said.

"Well, that's the point. My own little fun house." A hint of a smile appeared on Mercy's face, and then her lips drooped. "But I'm not having any fun tonight."

Louisa did not think anyone was. Not anymore. "We've been looking for you all over. You shouldn't have run off."

Mercy settled herself on a web. "I had to get out of there. I knew what everyone would think. That it was me causing mischief." Louisa did not tell her that was *exactly* what Darcelle had thought. "But you have to believe me! I didn't call that darkness."

Louisa had been sitting right beside Mercy, entranced by the performance. She didn't know what Mercy might have been up to with her shadow magic. If Mercy had meant to tease and prank Mina, as Ox had warned her *not* to do. If things had gone too far.

But no, Louisa may not have known Mercy long, yet she trusted her. And Mercy had a good heart. "I believe you," Louisa said.

Mercy frowned. "Well, you're the only one."

"That's not true. Ox and Jess know better too." Louisa

reached out tentatively, touching the web closest to her. It was soft, insubstantial, so unlike the needle points she'd felt earlier. "What sort of magic was that?"

"I don't know, but I didn't like the feel of it. Like pins and needles."

She had mirrored Louisa's thoughts. "It was almost like it wanted to cut out a piece of me. Something that doesn't like magic and wants to take it away," Louisa whispered, fearful the threads might be listening, twisting somewhere alongside Mercy's own shadows.

Mercy's hands tightened in her lap. Although it was dark, with the gold-flushed webbing Louisa could see Mercy's face well enough. Tears glittered in her eyes but did not fall. "Everyone will think it's me."

Louisa could no longer deny the rumors. "Maybe for now," she admitted, "but we will find who's behind it."

"I'm always frightening someone."

"What do you mean?"

A pause sat between them.

"I lost my parents long ago."

Louisa touched her heart, wondering if the love bugs drew nearer to Mercy, but if they approached, she could not hear them. "I'm sorry."

Mercy swallowed and then shared what she had not seemed ready to say before. "After they were gone, no one wanted to take me in. My shadows scared them. And then . . ." She looked down at her hands. "And then they did all they could to scare me. They lit torches to dispel the shadows. The whole town was alight day and night. I thought it would burn. I thought *I* might burn." Mercy raised her eyes. "It's only here at the carnival I've ever felt welcome. Or safe."

That wouldn't happen here. Louisa refused to let it. "It will be okay. I know it." Louisa meant every word, even if she didn't know how they could set things right.

From below, a ribbon of light speared into the tent. Darcelle appeared at the entrance, holding back the curtain. Under the seamstress's raised arm, Louisa could see Ox and Jess just outside, shuffling their feet guiltily.

Darcelle glanced up, catching sight of Louisa floating in the air and Mercy hunched in the web. Her red pile of hair blazed like a bonfire in the darkness. Mercy flinched.

"There you are, Mercedes," the seamstress said. "I was worried the shadows had stolen you away."

Darkness swarmed closer to Mercy, but Louisa thought it bundled her more like a blanket than a threat.

"Those shadows weren't mine," Mercy said, her voice low and defiant, as if Darcelle had just accused her of pulling Raven from the night-rope or breaking Mina's magic.

"Come down from there, darling." Darcelle's voice rang false, so sweet she might have dipped her tongue in sugar to lure Mercy to the ground. "Perhaps it was only some strange clash of magic?"

Mercy sniffed and wiped her eyes. "Not *my* magic." She looked like she wanted to disappear into the shadows again, but then she bowed her head and slipped down her silken threads of webbing.

"Wasn't it though? Fiona thinks we should all have a little talk," Darcelle said, eyes trained on Mercy. "And the rest of you ought to head to bed. It's been a very long day."

Louisa exhaled deeply, but she had even more trouble than usual controlling her mystique. It almost ached to call the magic needed for descent. Thinking it must only be fatigue, she grabbed hold of the nearest thread of webbing. Hand over hand, she lowered herself close to the ground.

She trailed after Mercy and, wanting to give her some last bit of encouragement, said, "Jess and I will wait up for you."

Setting her fingertips on Mercy's shoulder, Darcelle steered her away. "Who says she will be returning?"

ᴄ 23 ᴠ
GRIEF-HUNGRY LOVE BUGS

After all that had happened, Louisa thought she would have trouble sleeping, but slumber caught her as soon as she closed her eyes. She woke only once the sun was already high in the sky. Immediately, she rolled over, propping her elbow on the air just above the ground, and looked to the spot in the corner of the tent where Mercy always slept.

It was empty.

Her eyes flew to the opposite corner. Jess lay curled on her side, breathing deeply. Still asleep.

Louisa flopped back down. Although she had hoped to find Mercy snug in her lumpy blankets, Louisa remembered that she had once spent a night in Darcelle's beautiful tent. There was nothing to worry about. But she could not convince her stomach, which twisted into knots.

There had been so many strange occurrences, one right after another, including the storm that prevented her leaving. She'd thought the wind and the clouds had tangled like threads—threads so much like the ones she'd seen when Raven fell and when the sisters lost control of their act.

From her shoulder, she plucked up a strand of her hair, brushing her fingers across the silver ends. The ones that reminded her of Quiet Si.

Louisa sighed, tickling her chin with the tips of her hair. If Quiet Si's hair had not always been silver, she wondered what color it might have been. Neither fair nor ginger. Those shades did not match his coloring. She could almost picture him with hair the color of a starless midnight sky.

But it was a silly, fanciful thought.

Still, he might know something about the darkness overtaking the carnival. And Mercy needed her help.

◁ ★ ▷

Louisa found Quiet Si by the pond she'd first spied on her way through the Spark Woods. He stood at the end of the narrow pier, bent over one of the little boats. Sunlight fell on the water, sending golden ripples across its surface.

She made no sound as she approached, her feet floating just above the wooden planks, but he turned, perhaps sensing her presence by a gentle shift in the wind.

"Where did the butterflies go?" she asked, remembering the way they'd pulled the boat on threads of silver, much like the lines that tied the sky basket to the moon.

"They are made of the same fabric of magic as everything else. When they are not here, they are elsewhere." He glanced away, and Louisa thought he might be able to see into that other place even if she could not.

Louisa squinted into the sun. Despite the brightness of the autumn day, a cool wind blew across the water. The boats knocked gently against the pier.

"I was wondering," she said, and Quiet Si looked back at her. "I was wondering how your hair turned silver. You see, mine has changed as well."

The breeze blew her long strands into the air. Quiet Si reached out, touching the ends between two wooden fingers almost the way her mother had once done. He frowned and then let her hair drop back to her shoulders. "It was the day the stars fell. Have they fallen again?" He looked at her feet, as if a pile of stars might lie scattered on the ground.

"No," Louisa reassured him. "Are you talking of the day you lost your yesterdays and your name?" She used the same words he'd spoken before, hoping it would jar loose some memory.

"The sky was full of shadows, clouding the moon and my way," he said grimly. "They twisted everywhere."

Louisa's pulse jumped. Could he be talking about the

very thing that pulled Raven from her rope and chased the sisters—and Louisa—on the stage? Just like those malicious threads that tore after her during the storm? She felt so close to answers. If only he spoke more plainly, maybe she could understand. "What else do you remember?" she said softly, not wanting to interrupt his fragile hold on the past.

"I caught a star once," Si said. "She was beautiful."

"She?" Louisa asked, still unused to him referring to stars in this way. But it seemed he was already moving away from the things she most hoped to know.

"Oh yes, glittering and bright." He closed his pale eye; his wooden one remained open and unseeing. "How she loved to laugh."

"The star?" Louisa asked. Twinkling was so much like laughter, she could not fault his description.

"I should have kept her in my pocket." He shook his head, perhaps realizing he'd said something odd, but what he said next made no better sense. As if he were confusing the star-crackers made by Fire-Red Rosalyn with something else. "She should have kept me in her pocket."

Louisa was content to let him wind his stories wherever they would go, following along with him to the end, but when a line creased his forehead and his feet twitched on the ground, she worried she'd pushed him too far. Placing a hand on his arm, she said, "Stars belong in the sky, don't they?"

Si's eye opened once again. A look of relief washed over his face, a sign that she'd said just the right thing. "Of course they do," he agreed. "And so, all I have in my pockets is grief."

A familiar clicking sound, almost masked by the boats rocking against the pier, shivered through the air. Quiet Si patted the pockets of his striped coat, scaring loose a glossy black insect. It scrambled down, fast across his pant leg to the ground, where it quickly scuttled away.

Louisa's eyes grew round. In the daylight, there was no mistaking it.

A love bug.

She reeled back. "Why have you got them in your pockets?" Her voice trembled, and her thoughts ran wild, recalling when she'd heard those awful bugs chattering most recently. Each time, she'd been with Quiet Si. She'd wondered why they'd kept so close to her, but they must have been clinging to him all along.

"There is a hole of grief inside me. They help me remember her." A single tear dripped from his pale eye to his wooden cheek.

A fierce longing for her mother swept through Louisa. How she would have loved to ride a boat led by butterflies. How amazed she would have been to see Louisa dancing through the air in a leotard of gold. How much she would have enjoyed the fresh smell of the maples and their bright red leaves.

If only the grief-hungry love bugs had lived in her pockets instead of her heart.

"Who?" Louisa said, but she knew. She *knew*. He'd said his name was not his own, but maybe it was the only one he could remember. How had she not realized it before? Si was so much like Simone, a whisper of her mother's name. A name to honor the woman he loved and lost.

"The star, of course." He wiped his eye and turned back to the boats, tightening the knots that tethered them to the pier.

Louisa blinked. Hot tears welled in her eyes. That wasn't what he was supposed to say. He was supposed to say her mother's lovely name. He was supposed to tell her he was her father.

But how could he be? With his heavy wooden bones and his slow, steady gait, there was no one more sewn to the earth than he was. Louisa backed away, taking small steps, and then she turned and ran.

Tears pushed up, pushed past all the locks she'd wrapped around her heart. For weeks and weeks, she'd held them at bay. In a horrible rush, they streamed down her face. It seemed they would never stop.

But as she ran, the wind dried her eyes and her cheeks. Every part of her ached from their release. Inside, she felt so empty, and when she heard a click and a clack, she knew, this time, the love bug was coming after her.

She dashed away from it. She would not let it into her

pocket or her heart, which was so newly filled with love for Ox and Jess, Quiet Si too—and Mercy, who might have needed her most of all. No matter her own hurt, she had to be brave for them.

If Quiet Si had told her little (although she would not dismiss his ramblings about a sky full of twisting shadows), there was one person who likely knew more.

⋉ 24 ⋊
SHIFTING SHADOWS

Louisa stormed through the carnival and burst into her tent, where her friends had all gathered. Jess rested one hand on Mercy's arm, as if she'd been consoling her upon her return from Darcelle's. They startled at Louisa's appearance and her steely expression.

"Thank goodness you're back," she said to Mercy, who looked in the foulest of moods with a big grumpy frown and scrunched-together eyebrows. "We need to talk to Fiona. We need her to read your misfortune."

Mercy rounded her shoulders, sulking. "I already know my misfortune. Darcelle and Fiona told me I was not mindful of my magic. That I have never learned to tame it." Mercy's voice dropped low. "And now I am forbidden from using it."

"Forever?" Jess gasped.

"Maybe. If they don't figure out who's really been churning up the darkness and making a mess of everything."

"That isn't fair," Louisa said, jolted by the news. "And all the more reason to talk to Fiona and uncover what's behind these mishaps of magic."

"I don't want to," Mercy said stubbornly. "I have avoided it ever since I arrived here. What if she tells me something *worse*?"

"But what if she tells you something *better*?" Ox said. He glanced at Louisa, and she felt grateful that he'd so promptly agreed with her.

Jess's fingers tightened around Mercy's wrist. "It's the best idea we've had."

"It's the *only* idea we've had," Mercy grumbled.

"Well, it's decided, then," said Jess. "Let's go."

With a reluctant sigh of acceptance, Mercy followed Louisa and the others into the cool afternoon and all the way to Fiona.

When they reached the old tent, they found the curtain swept to the side, held back with a long, black sash. Louisa poked her head through the opening. The sun slanted in beside her, warming the trailing vines and framing Fiona in a square of light. She sat alone at her table, humming a melancholy tune as she readied flowers for Plum Square's market.

"Hello, Fiona," Louisa said, feeling less bold now

that she stood before the misfortune teller. There was no knowing what she might see.

"I thought you would come," Fiona said, gesturing Louisa and the others inside. Her gaze swept over them all, then fixed squarely on Mercy. "Though I may not have the answers you seek."

Mercy hesitated. "That's why I didn't want to come." All the same, she strode forward and slumped down in the only other chair in the tent. "But they made me."

Before Louisa could protest, Fiona's voice came sharp. "I can only speak to what I see, not what one wishes to hear. Hearing your misfortune is your choice alone. Do you want to see it? To glimpse it? To know what is to come?"

Mercy squirmed in her seat. Shadows darkened the tent's interior. "I guess so."

"We can wait outside." As much as Louisa hoped to hear what Fiona would foretell, she wasn't sure if Mercy wanted them there.

But Mercy glanced back, eyes wide. "Stay."

Louisa offered a small smile.

"We're here for you," Ox said.

"Very well," Fiona said, and Mercy turned back around.

A deep quiet settled around them. Fiona plucked a petal from a rose in the wooden bucket near her feet. She held it between her fingers and peered into Mercy's eyes. For many moments, she said nothing.

Still standing in the doorway, Louisa leaned into the sunlight warming her back, but it could not chase off the chill that slipped through her the longer Fiona remained silent. The misfortune teller's eyebrows drew together. Her mouth pinched tight. She picked another petal, from a different rose this time.

The tent grew darker still. Mercy's magic slipped loose, shifting shadows even though she'd been forbidden from doing so.

At last, Fiona tipped back in her chair. She shook her head.

Louisa leaned forward so as not to miss a word.

"What did you see?" Mercy whispered.

"I could not read your misfortune." Fiona ground the rose petals in her hand.

"Oh," Mercy said, sounding relieved.

"Isn't that a good thing?" A note of hope rang in Jess's voice.

"It is a worrisome thing. Mercy's eyes were veiled and would not tell me a thing." Fiona watched Mercy, as if she very much wanted to tear past whatever had clouded her vision.

Mercy turned in the chair, away from the intensity of Fiona's scrutiny, and faced Louisa, Ox, and Jess. "Anyone else want a go?" Her words fell lightly, but her eyes, usually a warm shade of brown, looked a matted black, hooded by shadows.

No wonder Fiona could not stare into their depths and glean a misfortune. Mercy seemed to have cloaked them. For the briefest of moments, before she smooshed the thought, Louisa again wondered if Mercy might be hiding something.

She let Mercy, Ox, and Jess file out of the tent ahead of her so they would not see her guilt-reddened cheeks in the sunlight—and because she had one last question for Fiona.

"Ease your mind, Louisa," Fiona said, coming out from behind her table and swishing her skirts of raspberry, forest green, and cobalt. "You are a ball of nerves. But I think it's more than Mercy's ill-fated telling that has you worried. What is it that troubles you? That burdens you? That keeps you from settling your heart?"

Louisa raised her head, letting her eyes catch the light. "Has my misfortune changed?"

Fiona only had to look at Louisa for a moment before she said, "I cannot tell you another misfortune, for the first one is not at its end."

"It is," Louisa insisted. The misfortune had already come to pass. She had not—she would not—find her father. No matter how much she wished it.

Fiona rubbed the crumpled petal between her fingers, as if to be sure. "I'm afraid not. So long as you still hold even the slimmest sliver of hope, you will have no other misfortune as great as this one, and I will perceive no others. Have you seen the other side of it? What I could not see?" She tilted her head. "What has your heart shown you?"

"Nothing," Louisa said, but her chest tightened. What she'd seen—that her father might find *her* instead—seemed like just another fancy.

That Quiet Si might be her father—was impossible.

It was best to accept that fate had taken her father from her forever, something her mother had never been able to believe.

25

THE WORST SORT OF TRICKERY

With darkened skies and pitch-black midnights, shadows closed in on the carnival. Or at least, that is what everyone whispered. Louisa knew better. As the days passed, it was only autumn marching dutifully forward, daylight giving way to the night more quickly as winter neared. Mercy's magic had nothing to do with it—at least Louisa did not *think* so.

But she did not feel entirely settled. A not-right feeling still lingered.

Raven refused to leave her tent, and not just because her leg and her magic were still mending. She kept a candle burning at all hours (just as the townsfolk who chased Mercy away had done), and she was not the only one shrinking from the shadows. Everyone had grown wary.

The threads of darkness sneaked about, spooking the

pale mare, snuffing out Fire-Red Rosalyn's flames during practice, and chasing poor, broken Mina again, as if it wanted a taste of both sisters' magic. It had probably done much more, but those were the only rumors Louisa had overheard—not for a lack of silent-footed snooping.

She listened outside tents (quick and quiet when she made her getaway) and floated up into the treetops (observing from afar). Her sneaking was the only good to come of it all, for it allowed her to practice her magic.

And it forced her to confront her continued inability to descend. Fear had no weight, no substance, but it held her aloft as surely as the wind.

One night after the shows, which thankfully went off without mishap or mistake, Louisa, Ox, Jess, and Mercy gathered in the girls' tent, talking over what they should do. No one—not Fiona, not Darcelle, not even Quiet Si—would tell them a thing, only reassuring them over and over again that everything would be okay and that nothing would harm them (all while watching Mercy with careful eyes). Louisa wanted to believe it, but there was no telling what might happen next.

Any day they might banish Mercy from the carnival. Especially because, though she'd been forbidden from using her magic, and therefore from performing, Mercy still called to her shadows in secret, sulking in the girls' tent as everyone else took to their stages.

"I heard Rosalyn say she would no longer go anywhere alone," Louisa said, frightened to note that when Rosalyn's fire had dimmed, so had her spirit. The very atmosphere of the carnival hung gloomy and brisk and mistrustful.

"What sort of trickery is it?" Jess might have been without magic, but she seemed no less determined to root out the source of the carnival's troubles.

"It is the worst sort." Ox magicked Louisa's red scarf from her small crate of belongings and flung it into the air above their heads. It coiled and lengthened in turn—like a snake. "The kind that's able to slip through the fingers of my mind. I can't grab hold of it."

Mercy, who had been quiet much of the night, focused her dark eyes on Louisa. "Did you bring it with you when you came? Or, might it have followed you into the carnival from the woods?" The scarf drooped to the ground. "None of this started happening until you arrived."

Everyone fell silent and turned to Louisa. Her heart clattered around in her chest, but when she pushed past her initial hurt, she could see that Mercy was not accusing her of anything. She was only asking a question they should have considered before.

"I . . . I do not think so," Louisa said, but that didn't mean the events were unrelated.

"So it is possible that you brought this trouble," Mercy said.

Louisa felt cornered, and perhaps that is how Mercy felt too, as if she had to deflect the blame at any cost. It gave Louisa the courage to ask what she'd previously held back for fear of offending Mercy. "Why did you not want Fiona to read your misfortune? Is there something you haven't told us?"

Mercy fiddled with a pin in her hair and looked everywhere but at Louisa, Ox, and Jess. "I just—" She bit off whatever she had planned to say. Her shadows rippled the air, a sign that her emotions tumbled wild. "I thought you trusted me. But you *don't!*"

Before Louisa could respond, Mercy jumped up and bolted out of the tent. The shadows slithered after her, like a cape made of night.

"Oh no," Jess said.

"I—I didn't mean . . . ," Louisa stammered. She wasn't at all sure what she'd meant, what she'd thought. "I only—"

A horrified shout cut off the rest of her words.

"What was that?" Jess practically jumped into Louisa's lap in her fright.

"The darkness strikes again," Ox said ominously. The three of them looked at the empty space Mercy had so recently filled.

Already floating inches off the ground, Louisa was the first to her feet. "Come on. Come quick. Someone's in trouble."

Ox parted the curtain ahead of them, and they tore into the night. The cold swept over Louisa, who in her haste had not taken the time to grab her coat. They ran down one row of tents and then another, past the worried faces of the carnival workers peeking out at the commotion. The cry came again, less sharp this time but no less anguished.

As they rounded the next corner, they stopped all at once. A group had already gathered outside one of the many small tents that served as living quarters. Louisa craned her neck, trying to determine whose it might be.

"They'll see us," Ox hissed, tugging her away without touching her. "And then they'll send us off as they always do."

"They won't." Stepping from the darkness, Mercy appeared beside them. She cast shadows around Louisa, Ox, and Jess.

"You're okay." Louisa was relieved Mercy had not been the one to scream. But all the same, she wondered what Mercy might have been up to in those brief moments she'd been alone in the night.

They crept toward the tent from the rear. As they drew closer, they heard voices.

"Talk more slowly. Tell us exactly what happened." Louisa recognized Darcelle's tone and the silhouette of her towering hair through the tent's walls.

"I don't know. I don't know," said an agonized male voice. "Just help her!"

A stretch of quiet followed the outcry, and it worried Louisa all the more. She dared to shift herself closer, slipping around the trunk of an old maple. The clouded breaths of her friends puffed forward as they too gathered nearer.

"Lovely Valentine," whispered the third person outlined in the tent. Fiona.

Louisa shared a look with Ox. She could not imagine what tragedy might have befallen the Living Tattoo.

"Is she moving? Is she breathing? Can you sense her pulse of life?" Fiona rattled off her questions, a nervous hitch spiking each one louder than the one before.

When Fiona paused and Bubba Wild (who must have been the one to scream) did not immediately reply, Louisa's mind went to the darkest places. She pictured Valentine lifeless and still, inked arms crossed atop her inked chest, a pair of black *X*s marked over her eyes. It was a horrible thought. It could not be true.

"What happened?" Darcelle said again, more urgently.

"The shadows came, just as Fiona said they would." Bubba Wild's voice shuddered. "And now Lovely Valentine is *fading*." He began weeping and said no more.

The truth was hardly better than Louisa's imaginings. What if Lovely Valentine disappeared entirely?

Louisa sucked in a terrified breath, drifting away from the ground. Her head tapped a low hanging branch, shaking loose leaves. They showered down on the tent's rooftop. Mercy glared up at her while Jess yanked the hem of her dress and pulled her back to the ground. Wide-eyed, Louisa brushed crumbling leaves from her hair.

"What was that?" The silhouette of Darcelle's hair wobbled as she tipped back her head.

"I will check on it," Fiona replied.

In unspoken agreement, Louisa and her friends slunk away from the tent and scurried back to the girls' own before Fiona could spot them. They fell through the doorway, scrambling into the places they'd been sitting only minutes ago.

"I'm sorry," Louisa said. She had almost gotten all of them caught. She eyed the tent's entrance, but no one came.

"Never mind that." Mercy waved away the apology. "Did you hear what Bubba Wild said?"

"'Course we did." Jess shook her head solemnly. "Lovely Valentine is fading. The poor, poor thing."

Louisa looked at her own hands, so solidly skin and bone. To be made of ink seemed such a strange thing, and for those lines to fade a nightmare. For all the tragedy that had struck the carnival, none had been worse than this. Someone's life was coming undone. "Why are the threads set on destroying magic?"

Jess gasped. "They aren't."

"But they are. They have."

"Oh, the darkness is *taking* the magic all right, but not to do away with it. To keep it!" Jess ran her fingers through the air and then made a snatching motion. "I mean, that's what I'd do. I'd steal it for myself."

"Jess!" Louisa's mouth dropped open.

"Not that I did, of course."

"That *must* be what's happening," Ox said, talking fast. "Someone in the carnival is a thief!"

Louisa tugged at the ends of her hair. The silver tips seemed even more worrisome now. Had someone not just injured her magic, but stolen a pinch of it too?

Mercy frowned at each of them in turn. "Yes, all of that. But Bubba Wild said something else as well."

A shiver ran down Louisa's spine as she recalled his words. She recited them exactly, "'The shadows came, just as Fiona said they would.'"

Mercy threw shadows around them, mimicking the dark threads. "What if it's her? What if Fiona is not a *Teller* of Misfortune?" The shadows swirled faster and faster, sinking Mercy's face into darkness. "What if she is a *Bringer* of Misfortune?"

⟲ 26 ⟳
SNARE THE BUTTERFLY

A thief lived among them.

Louisa hated to even think it—that Fiona might have been the one controlling the threads of darkness and stealing snippets of magic. It hardly seemed possible that someone as kind as Fiona would do such a thing. Unless she offered phony smiles and false warmth, misleading everyone she met.

The more the idea tumbled around Louisa's mind, the stronger it took hold. After all, Fiona was the one who had left the invitations luring those with magic and mystiques to the carnival. She was the one who could look into someone's eyes and cast a misfortune. Who knew what else she could pull from her hair besides flowers?

"Fiona?" Louisa whispered. "But why?"

And why *now*? Mercy's earlier questions bounced

around in her head—if Louisa's arrival had somehow sparked everything. She could see no connection. She did not want to see a connection. Yet the twisting in her belly told her not to ignore the possibility.

"I don't know," Mercy admitted, a frown on her face.

Without raising so much as his hand or even his eyebrow, Ox lifted and lowered a jar of golden powder Jess had left out. It toppled over, sprinkling glitter, when he suddenly sat straight, mind shifting focus, and said, "Maybe she sells stolen magic in Plum. Did you see anything strange when you were there?" He turned to Jess, who had gone to the market with Fiona soon after the magic-touched windstorm blew through.

Louisa hoped Jess would tell him no. She did not want Fiona to be the thief. But even worse, she supposed, was thinking the thief might be Mercy.

Jess bent her knees and folded her arms around them, tugging her lip. "I don't think so, but I wasn't paying much attention. There was too much else to look at in Plum and so many errands to run."

"She probably sent you away on purpose so you wouldn't see what she was up to," Mercy said.

Deep in thought, Jess tipped her head to the side. "How do you bottle magic anyway?"

"Very carefully," said a voice from behind. The wind whistled at their backs, and they spun around to find Fiona standing at the tent's entrance—as if by talking of her they had summoned her.

Jess released a shriek-like giggle.

A marigold bloomed on the tip of Fiona's hair. Louisa watched its orange petals flush open and then fall to the ground, where they immediately withered. It did not seem a good sign.

"What is this talk of bottling magic?" Fiona's eyes flew over each of them in turn, lingering on Mercy and landing last on Louisa. Perhaps Fiona thought the others might fib and Louisa might give her the truth.

Jess, Ox, and Mercy stared at Louisa, waiting to see how she would answer Fiona's question. Louisa shook with nerves, but instead of taming the worry, she let it flood her, pretending they didn't already know what had happened to Lovely Valentine. Anything to deflect attention from what they'd just been talking about. "Fiona, what's happened? We heard someone cry out."

"Oh yes," Fiona said, distracted from her questioning. The glimmer of sadness in her eyes looked genuine, but Louisa didn't know whether to trust it or not. Everyone at the carnival was a performer after all. "That is why I came. I'm afraid Lovely Valentine has . . . taken ill."

Jess clasped her hands together. "No! She has?" All wide-eyed and open-mouthed, Jess quite overdid the surprise, Louisa thought, but Fiona seemed not to notice.

"Don't worry. Don't fret. Don't concern yourselves at all. She will be all right. Everything is fine." A carnation tumbled from Fiona's hair as easily as the lies from her lips.

Everything was *not* fine.

When Raven had fallen, Louisa first witnessed Fiona sprouting flowers uncontrolled, and they fell too when she'd rushed in after Mina's misadventure on stage. Once, Louisa might have thought worry prompted the flowers to bloom in this manner, but now, she wondered if it might have more to do with some dark magic—no matter their sweet fragrance and delicate petals.

Fiona nudged the flower aside with the heel of her boot. "Ox, let me walk you back to your tent. It's time everyone got some shut-eye, I should think."

"I can walk myself," he said, scoffing at the offer. But his golden eyes flickered. He probably did not want to be alone with Fiona, and Louisa did not blame him.

"I insist," Fiona replied.

Ox stumbled to his feet and bundled into his coat. Before he left, he spun round to face Louisa, Mercy, and Jess. Out of sight of Fiona, he flashed them big eyes and grimacing lips, a goofy face of fright that might have made Louisa laugh in other circumstances. But Mercy had placed that glimmer of doubt into her head, and until she knew otherwise, she would be cautious of Fiona.

"We will see you tomorrow," Louisa said, a promise to Ox, a warning to Fiona.

Once they had gone, Mercy peeked into the night, watching them as long as she could.

Jess flopped back on the ground, an arm slung over her face. "What if she sucks the magic right out of his bones?"

Mercy shushed her. "She wouldn't dare. It would be too obvious if she took it tonight since we know she's gone off with him."

"What if she does dare? What if she drains every last drop of Ox's magic and then slips back to our tent hungry for *yours*?" Jess whispered.

"I'd like to see her try." Mercy's jaw tightened.

Although Louisa could not shake her worry for Ox, she placed her trust in Mercy. Trust that she'd let waver and needed to gather again. She picked up her red scarf, which Ox had dropped earlier, and hugged it to her chest. "Mercy, if you are right about Fiona, then we must do something about it."

"Should we tell someone? Should we tell Darcelle?" Jess peeked from underneath her elbow like a mouse sticking its nose out from a tiny hole in the wall.

"Not until we know for sure." Louisa thought about how hasty she'd been to imagine Quiet Si her father. And how foolish. She did not want to falsely accuse Fiona.

"Whoever it is, they seem to be getting more careful, stealing the magic when no one else is around. We need to set a trap of some sort."

Mercy smiled. "Like catching a butterfly in a spider's web."

Louisa flinched at the comparison, but it was exactly right. "Yes, something like that."

Although Fiona had told them to sleep, they stayed up another hour, thinking of what to do. Only when they'd agreed on a plan did they crawl to their separate pallets, set their heads to their pillows, and snuggle into their blankets.

"Good night," said Louisa, blowing out the candle beside her.

"Good night," said Mercy and Jess, who'd already put out their own small flames.

Lying there in the darkness, even as her friends' breaths became heavy with slumber, Louisa could not sleep. Too many thoughts jumbled in her head. She worried if the plan would work and if Ox was truly okay, but more than that kept her awake. Right then, she missed her mother very much.

As quiet as could be, she relit the candle, which was no more than a stub and cast only a small ring of light, and then she reached for her bag. Inside, she found her book and pulled it onto her lap. It was the closest thing to her mother she had, a comfort still and always. Louisa cracked it open. As usual, it fell to a place somewhere in the middle, so she flipped backward to the very first page.

Long ago, after her mother had found Louisa admiring the spine, hesitant to lift it from the shelf without permission, her mother had taken it down and written Louisa's name there next to her own, marking its owners. "It is not only mine; it is *our* book," her mother had said, something they could share and treasure. Louisa loved the curled script her mother used to form her letters, and now, she very much wanted to touch the ink, so worried it might have faded like the outline of Lovely Valentine.

Looking down at the page, she breathed a sigh of relief. The black script did not show any signs of aging, at least not yet, and Louisa brushed her finger over her mother's name and then her own. Below them, another hand had scrawled a line. She'd almost forgotten that her father had gifted the book to her mother. Tilting the page to the flickering candlelight, she read the simple line:

For the star who brightens my life. —William LaRoche

Louisa traced the letters of his name too and smiled. This little book held such a small piece of her family between the pages, but their names on the paper meant everything to her. Even if they were not beside her, these pages held their love.

◁ ★ ▷

The next morning, Louisa, Jess, and Mercy waited for Ox at the edge of the Spark Woods. When he appeared, Jess tackled him in a hug, as if she hadn't been sure he'd come all in one piece, magic intact.

But his magic was quite clearly intact, for he used it to extract himself from Jess's arms, lifting her off him and twirling her in a circle that soon had her giggling. Reassured that he was fine, Louisa and her friends tucked themselves away from prying ears and eyes. Away from Fiona, so she could not hear of their plans.

"Snare the Butterfly?" Ox asked after they had explained everything (including the very official name Jess had insisted upon calling it). A scowl darkened his face. "You aren't supposed to come up with ideas without me."

"Well, we did," Mercy said.

"And it's a good one," Jess added.

Louisa was not so sure about that, but then, she would be at the very center of the trap, luring the darkness to her, so of course she was more nervous than the others. "It doesn't matter whose idea it was. We need you too." Louisa suspected what worried Ox most of all was feeling left out. "You'll help us, won't you?"

"Of course, I will." Ox twisted his mouth to the side. "Now who is the butterfly again?"

"The thief—" Louisa began.

"Fiona is the butterfly," Mercy interjected, a certainty on her face about Fiona's devious intentions.

"Very well, *Fiona*." Louisa still had trouble getting used to the idea even though she'd thought of little else as she fell asleep the night before.

Ox looked over his shoulder and then leaned closer to them. "And who is the spider?"

"We are the spiders." Excitement rippled through Jess's voice. Though she would be doing nothing more than hiding and watching, she'd taken to the role, as if it came with a dusting of magic.

"Shh!" Mercy hissed.

"When?" Ox's mouth curved up at the corner, his mood quickly improving.

"Tonight," Mercy said. Her brown eyes glinted as bright and fiery as the Spark Woods, a certainty within them that she would clear her name.

◁ ★ ▷

However, for three nights in a row, as Louisa practiced, no threads of darkness appeared. Oh, but the reminders of them were everywhere. The candle glow from Raven's tent at all hours, Mina's sobbing when the sisters still could not combine, and the ever-present fear that Lovely Valentine would be erased from existence.

On the fourth evening, Louisa entered the roofless big top alone once again. Though it looked much the same as it normally did, clouds blotted out the stars, casting overlarge shadows into the corners and under the benches. Of course, shadows were not the only things hiding in the gloom. Somewhere, Mercy and Ox crouched out of sight.

She walked to the very center of the tent, avoiding looking at the shadows too directly. Best she did not know precisely where her friends had tucked themselves or she might spoil their hiding places. As for Jess, she watched Fiona's tent, reasoning that since she had no magic, Fiona would not be likely to pay her any mind or feel her close presence.

From beyond the tent came the chirping of crickets, which served as Louisa's music in place of the cello. She inhaled a breath and took to the air, floating around in a circle, arms outstretched. Nothing fancy, nothing that would distract her, for she needed to remain watchful. The threads of darkness were out there somewhere. And tonight, they might come for her magic.

Fiona might come for her magic.

Just thinking of it made her nervous. She'd intercepted the threads of darkness before. Although they'd barely grazed her, she hadn't forgotten their sharp touch. Or what they'd done to her hair. She was not looking forward to encountering them again.

Lost in her head, Louisa had drifted close to the south wall of the tent and spun herself away from it, tugging her thoughts back with her. She needed to focus.

Above, the clouds shifted, revealing a crescent moon.

It barely brightened the sky, the sliver of it was so slim. But there was enough light shining down to see the thread of darkness breaking from the shadows and slithering toward her.

Midair, Louisa froze.

Although she'd been waiting for just this moment, it came without warning. Her eyes tore around the tent, searching for some sign of Fiona, but there was only the magical thread whispering closer and the faintest clinking of wind chimes. She dashed away, pretending she could fly swiftly and ably. Behind her, it slunk back and forth. And then it whipped forward, twining up her ankles before she could dart away, slipping over her wrists, seeping through skin and bone and tissue. Pins and needles ran through her body.

It dug deeper, cutting into her very core.

Louisa shrieked and shrieked. Uncontrolled, she spiraled downward. Never before had she descended so quickly. Her stomach heaved, as if she'd left it twenty feet up in the air.

The ground rushed toward her face.

L ouisa could not breathe, the air plucked from her lungs by the swath of darkness. In rebellion, her arms flailed. Her legs kicked. Head over heels she went, heart pounding, eyes blurring with wind. The sky and earth flipped upside down, as if the ground rose above her and the stars fell at her side.

She flung her hands over her face and squeezed shut her eyes, imagining her body touching the ground for the very first time and shattering—like Darcelle Duval's red crystal chandelier—into a thousand shards that could never be put back together.

With what little strength she had left, she sucked in a shaky breath. It ached like the sharpest autumn air. A great weight caught hold of her limbs—Ox's quick grasp—and a soft shadow enveloped her—Mercy's speedy cushioning.

They buoyed her at the very last moment. Her body jerked with the sudden shift in momentum, and her eyes flew open against her will.

For all her twisting as she fell, she floated horizontally, facedown. Limbs limp, hair dangling on the ground, she could have kissed the dirt she had stopped so close above it.

"Louisa! Louisa!" Ox and Mercy burst from their hiding places and raced toward her. All she could see of them was their boots kicking up dust.

When they reached her, they clasped her shoulders, helping her upright. She was too weak to do it herself.

Louisa touched a hand to her brow, then her chest, still not quite believing she was all in one piece. "I don't feel very well," she admitted, dizzy-headed. She'd never thought she could fall, and the idea that she *had* fallen rattled her. They led her to a bench, where she sat just above it, trembling. It took all her effort to speak. "I thought I would be broken apart."

"So did I," Ox said, but for once, she wished he had not agreed with her so quickly.

"I'm frightened," she said softly, reaching for the hum of her magic, which felt so distant, so fragile. "Is my magic all gone?"

Mercy and Ox looked her over, but of course, they could not see the whole of her magic. It was inside her.

"You're still floating," Mercy said.

"You're still magical," Ox added.

Louisa clung to their reassurances. With wide eyes, she peered around the tent. "Did you see anyone?" Her near-death experience, the weakening of her magic, it had to at least be worth something.

Ox and Mercy flicked their eyes at each other and then turned back at Louisa.

"I saw no one," Ox said.

"I saw nothing," Mercy confirmed.

They had probably been too busy watching Louisa tumble from the sky, stretching their own magic to keep her from crashing. "Neither did I." All she'd seen were those smoky threads. All she'd heard were the delicate notes of the wind chime.

Although she'd hardly spoken, she felt out of breath, like she'd just run circles around the entire carnival. Spots danced before her eyes. Or were they stars? She blinked to clear her vision.

"You look awfully pale." Ox scooted back a step, as if she might throw up at his feet.

Louisa held her belly, determined not to be sick, and glanced up at her friends' concerned faces. "It feels as though little pieces of myself have been snipped away," she whispered. Little pieces of her magic.

A breeze wheeled through the open roof of the big top. Louisa braced herself, but the gust snatched her up, and no matter how she called to her magic to keep herself grounded, it did not answer. All her practicing had been for nothing. Her heart beat madly.

Mercy and Ox yanked her back to them and settled her on the bench once more. Ox's hand remained on her shoulder.

For all she had learned and improved, her grasp on her magic had drifted out of reach—she had the sense that she could no more control her floating than she could call the shadows or breathe fire or lift a pebble with her mind. "It *is* gone!" Louisa cried.

"Not gone," Ox said. "Just . . . some part of it has gone missing."

Mercy looked up and all around, as if Louisa's magic might be tingling in the air above them, something she could collect and return, the way she gathered her shadows. "It was Fiona, bringing misfortune." Mercy's face hardened. "We have to talk to Jess."

"Only if Fiona hasn't cast a misfortune on her too," Ox said.

"We shouldn't have left her alone this long." Mercy snatched a shadow from beneath her boot, and she flung it up into the sky, a dark spot against the gray clouds. With a twirl of her fingers, she sent it zipping into the night.

"What was that?" Louisa's skin prickled the way it might if love bugs had run across it.

"A messenger." When Louisa stared at her blankly, Mercy added, "The shadow will tug Jess back to me."

"Oh!" Louisa had seen Mercy perform many tricks, but not this one. As much as it impressed her, it also frightened her. She did not want to think about shadows tugging; it was much too close to what she'd experienced this very night.

"Come on, we'll meet her halfway." Mercy marched away from them before Louisa could ask more.

"Do you feel well enough to walk?" Ox leaned forward, a gesture that implied he intended to *carry* her, and she stood quickly. That much, at least, she could manage.

"Yes, yes," she said, but Ox held out his hand when she wobbled and so she took it. Only the thinnest scrap of space kept her feet from the ground. Her magic had smooshed completely flat.

They followed Mercy out of the tent, hurrying down the pathways until they spotted Jess ahead, her blond hair bright in the darkness. She waved like she'd been away from them for ages, not hours. As they drew closer, Louisa noticed a shadow wrapped around Jess's wrist, leading her as someone might walk an overeager puppy. Jess's body jerked forward, and she laughed and frowned in turn.

"Oh my gosh, Mercy, you sent the bossiest gob of a messenger ever." Jess wedged her thumb between her wrist and the shadow, trying to peel it off. It yielded only when

Mercy snapped her fingers, unwinding and blending into the night.

"Just like Mercy herself." Ox snickered.

Louisa was so happy to see Jess teasing and laughing, untouched by whatever dark magic had swept through the big top, that she let her fingertips drop from Ox's hand and hugged Jess tight. "You're okay?"

Jess squeezed her back. "'Course I am. Another night of nothing!"

"What do you mean?" Louisa pulled back. This night had been the opposite of nothing. They had certainly stirred up *something*.

Something terrible.

"Shh. Never know who's listening." Mercy shooed them forward, and they quickened their pace to the girls' tent. Before Ox could sweep the curtains aside, she pushed through them, drawing them closed again once everyone slipped past. Hands on her hips, Mercy asked, "How did Fiona do it?"

"Do what? All she did was cut dead leaves from the vines, read to herself, and then she went to sleep. I thought spying would be fun, but it's boring beyond measure." Jess covered her mouth in an exaggerated fake yawn.

"She told no misfortunes? Flowers didn't drop like mad from her hair?" If Fiona hadn't been the one to release the darkness, Louisa was glad, of course, but it left them with a still-unsolved mystery. Louisa had risked her life, her magic, and the thief had bested them. She swayed on her feet.

"No, none of that," Jess grumped.

Mercy paced, scowling and seemingly unready to admit Fiona wasn't the culprit. "I thought for sure it was her. Maybe she can cast magic in her dreams?"

"Who else could it be?" Ox asked.

"Wait, did something happen? What did I miss?" Jess's gaze darted from Mercy to Ox, finally landing on Louisa.

With a tentative hand, Louisa pulled a long lock of hair over her shoulder and held it out so they all could see. Mercy froze when she saw it.

In the candlelight, the ends gleamed silver. The deadened strands had climbed another inch up Louisa's hair.

"Oh no!" Jess flinched away, as if the silver would leap through the air and drain the color from her own golden strands.

"Let's cut them off," Mercy said, fast with a solution. "Darcelle will have scissors."

Louisa gripped the tips in her fist. She did not want to lose the very ends her mother had last touched. And anyway, she did not think doing so would suddenly flood her body with magic. "I can't cut it."

"You'd better." Ox made a snipping motion with his fingers. "Otherwise you'll soon look like Quiet Si."

"It's probably him stealing the magic. Maybe this is how he marks his victims." Mercy glared at Louisa's hair.

Louisa wrapped her arms around her stomach, the queasy feeling getting worse instead of better. She knew Mercy was only grasping for someone else to blame, but this accusation felt so very wrong. "It is *not* Quiet Si. Don't say that!" Louisa had never raised her voice so firmly.

Mercy's mouth snapped shut.

Louisa glanced away.

Ox and Jess shared a look and a shrug.

Hurrying across the tent so she did not have to see the hurt in Mercy's eyes, Louisa dropped to her knees in front of her small crate of belongings and pulled out her bag. At the very bottom rested her mother's traveling sewing kit. She had brought it for remembrance, and the first glimpse of it warmed her as she opened the wicker lid. Everything rested tidily in the small compartments—glossy threads in a rainbow of colors, a set of fine needles, spare buttons and small patches, and even a miniature pair of scissors.

She lifted the sharp blades, stood once again, and held them out to Mercy. A peace offering of sorts. "Cut it."

"All right." Mercy did not hesitate. "But let's not make a mess in here." She pulled Louisa outside, and Jess and Ox darted out of the tent after them.

Squeezing shut her eyes, Louisa turned her back. In

Mercy's hand, the blades snip, snip, snipped, and the very ends of Louisa's hair sprinkled to the ground.

Louisa sighed. It wasn't as bad as she'd thought. It was only hair after all. It would regrow, and maybe her magic would too. She began to turn around.

Mercy held her in place with a hand to her shoulder. "Wait!" The scissors clipped again and again.

When Mercy stopped, Louisa spun around, sweeping her hair over her shoulder. "Why did you snip so much?" But Mercy did not answer, for as they watched, silver slipped up the very dark strands. If Louisa did not know better, she'd have thought that the ends had never been cut.

She dropped her hands, as if poison coated her hair.

Jess let out a shaky scream and then covered her mouth. "Sorry. It's just so . . . *strange*."

"It's more than strange," Ox said. "It's sinister."

Louisa swallowed hard. She shook her head.

"Like a spreading sickness," Mercy said, and handed Louisa the scissors.

Louisa would have liked to snip away Mercy's words, but they echoed in her head. With a shaking hand, she slid the scissors into the pocket of her coat.

The whisper of slippered feet hurried down the path. "What's happened? Who cried out?"

All four of them turned at the sound of Darcelle's voice. Holding her long crimson skirts away from the dirt, she slipped closer, falling in and out of shadows cast by the windblown clouds. They made it impossible to read her mood. One moment, when the starlight caught her face, she looked wide-eyed with worry, and in the next moment, the night shaded her features, and she looked pinch-mouthed with secrets.

Fiona followed, more careful of where she stepped, as she wore no shoes. "Is someone hurt? Is there trouble? What tragedy has befallen the night?" Flowers fell from her hair and piled around her bare feet, as if she'd risen from her slumber and come in such a hurry, she'd given no thought to the cold. "Someone heard shouting by the big top, but no one was there when we arrived. And we heard another scream just now."

"Everything's fine," Ox said, standing in front of Louisa and blocking her from too close an inspection. But in doing so, Darcelle and Fiona only looked at her more intently, drawn to what Ox hoped to hide.

Louisa rubbed her cheeks to put some color into them and peeked around him. "Perfectly fine."

"We were goofing, is all," Mercy said. She kicked at the ground, stirring leaves and dirt.

"I fear you've done much more than that." Darcelle reached out, forcing Ox to the side with the sweep of her skirts, and brushed the silver ends of Louisa's hair with her fingertips.

Fiona's bellflowers turned to daisies. "The silvered shadows? The darkness?" She looked at Mercy. "A spider casting webs?"

"It wasn't Mercy!" Louisa said, worry tightening her throat.

Fiona ignored Louisa's plea. "Your magic has gone wild and uncontrolled." She touched the flowers in her hair, one after the other. "I see only more destruction ahead."

Darcelle came forward and circled her fingers around Mercy's wrist. "Fiona, we ought . . ."

"Yes, we ought, we should, we *will* set things right." Fiona frowned.

Darcelle nodded her head, a thin strand slipping free of her elaborate tower of hair and twirling and reaching in the breeze. "Come along now, without fuss or argument."

"I didn't do it!" Mercy cried, a desperately high pitch to her voice.

"Be truthful, now." Fiona rubbed a petal between her fingers.

Mercy's shoulders sagged. She cast sorrowful eyes at Louisa, Ox, and Jess, as if it might be the last time she saw them, and then she forced out, "My shadows have always obeyed me. I-I think they have at least!" She tripped over her words. "Haven't they?" Her voice trembled and broke, and she let Darcelle lead her away, head down, each footfall defeated.

Louisa stepped forward, ready to chase after them, but Mercy's words held her still, as did Fiona's steadying hand. "What did she say?" Out of sorts from all that had happened, Louisa must not have heard her correctly.

"I'm sure it was not purposeful. Mastering magic is no easy task." Fiona squeezed her shoulder. "What did the shadows take from you?"

Louisa shook her head, a signal for Ox and Jess to keep their mouths shut too. "I am fine. Truly."

But she was not.

Beneath the mottled sky of clouds and stars, Louisa thought of Mercy's earlier hesitation to tell them why she did not want her misfortune told, how her hair did not silver even though she'd felt the shadows' pins-and-needles touch in Mina's tent, her insistence that Fiona was a bringer of misfortune and the thief of the carnival's magic (and then quickly accused Quiet Si when they realized Fiona was not to blame).

Of course, most troublesome was Mercy's absolute and magnificent control of the shadows. And what it might mean if they truly had disobeyed her.

⋎ 28 ⋌
ALL THINGS LOST & BROKEN

Late into the night, long after Fiona had gone, Louisa dreamed of shadows and darkness. Someone held her hand, guiding her through gray clouds. It made her feel less afraid. Though she never saw a face in the dreamscape, Louisa knew Mercy was her lifeline.

The farther they walked among the shadows, the less sure-footed they became and the more distance crept between them. It was the doubt, wiggling in Louisa's head, pushing them apart, until, at last, Mercy's hand slipped away.

And then nothing at all tethered Louisa.

Through silvered air, she began an endless downward spiral, falling and falling and falling with the upturned stars. Another hand reached out, one with three fingers of skin and bone, and two of wood, but they could not stretch far enough.

She startled awake, snapped from the nightmare just

before crashing to the earth, but she knew what terrible fate had awaited her if she'd landed.

Her magic would break. Her bones would shatter.

And though the fallen stars would return to the sky, no one would be able to mend her—not unless they somehow magicked her together. She pictured herself much like Quiet Si, part girl, part marionette. A patchwork of skin and bone and wood.

Even in the light of early morning and the safety of her cozy tent, she shuddered. How strange it was to think of herself that way, and to imagine the stars at her feet instead of twinkling in the sky. She hadn't understood Quiet Si before, but her dream seemed much the same as the day he had lost his yesterdays and his name. As if he'd been in the air, not on the ground, when that long-ago storm of darkness blew through.

As if he'd crashed to the earth.

His magic broken. His bones shattered.

Louisa's blood chilled at the thought. She clutched her blankets. All the loose ends tangling in her mind started to tie together in a pattern she'd never expected.

If Quiet Si's abilities had been stolen, it explained so much about him. Maybe he'd been filled with magic long ago, a very special kind—the sort she'd been looking for when she first arrived at the carnival. Had he once walked upon the air instead of the earth?

Louisa's heart thundered. Jess tossed in her bedding, and Louisa could not help but think that Jess heard each fast beat.

But Louisa hardly noticed her. She could picture Quiet Si in her mind so clearly, floating from the third-floor window of her old apartment building and following the winds north. In the heart of the Spark Woods, someone might have tugged him from the sky, where his poor body smashed on the ground and could only be mended with new limbs of wood. He might have hit his head so hard his memories fled him. He might have been drained of magic, hair turned silver all at once.

If her imaginings were true, Mercy could not be to blame, no matter what anyone thought. The threads of darkness had come in the past, before Mercy had been born. Someone else was the thief, then and also now. And Quiet Si might be Louisa's father after all.

She'd thought so before and had doubted and disbelieved, but now, she felt such certainty—even as her head spun and spun, spots dancing in her vision.

Like falling stars.

Louisa scrambled for her mother's book, which she'd left by her bedside. She opened it to the first page with all their inked names and read her father's dedication again, finding meaning she hadn't seen before.

For the star who brightens my life.

"Oh my." Her hands shook. "Oh goodness."

Quiet Si talked of stars endlessly! *She is the brightest*, he'd said. Louisa had thought it an odd sort of remark, but maybe it was the sweetest sort of endearment for her mother. Gently, she set the book aside. She sat there a moment, everything sinking in, and then could hold still no more.

Louisa kicked back her blankets, dressing faster than she'd ever done before, and raced out of the tent without so much as a backward glance for Jess, who groggily called after her. "Where are you going so early?"

"To seek my misfortune!"

The sun was a faded blot above, caught behind thick clouds. It smelled like rain. It looked like gloom. But the weather could not dampen Louisa's spirit. She wrapped her red scarf once more around her neck, so bright, like her hope.

Louisa had never gone to Quiet Si's tent before, but she knew which one was his, and approached it, nerves aflutter. It was like she would be meeting him for the very first time. When she reached the tent, she stopped in front of the entrance, not quite knowing what to say. She whispered, "Quiet Si. It's Louisa."

There was no response. Not even when she called again, louder.

He must have risen even earlier than she had, but she

didn't know where he might have gone. And she had to, she just *had to* see him. She'd been without a father all her life, and she couldn't wait a moment more.

Louisa circled round and round the carnival. All the while, she wondered what he would say, what he would think when she told him what she'd discovered. Might he remember the past and her mother? She could not contain her excitement. It hummed through her, filling in the tiny spaces that had felt absent of magic.

But no matter where she looked, she could not find him. Fiona's misfortune was determined to be true. Yet, it was the first time Louisa understood it so clearly. Fiona hadn't said she wouldn't find her *father*. She'd said Louisa wouldn't find who she was looking for.

And Quiet Si was not at all who she'd expected.

The other side of the misfortune, the one her heart had shown her, was true as well. *He'd* found *her*! The very first night she'd arrived, he'd returned her bag to her as she twirled beneath the stars, hoping her mother was watching.

Louisa changed course, hurrying toward Fiona's tent—Fiona, who'd been so right about everything. Now that her innocence had been proven, she was the next-best person to tell. But when Louisa arrived, there was no sign of the misfortune teller.

The wind blew gently. It gathered the clouds closer and batted at Louisa's scarf. The fuzzy tassels whipped up, tickling her cheek, reminding her of who'd gifted it. Louisa squared her shoulders and hurried toward Darcelle's tent. Maybe Mercy would be there too, and they could set things right all at once.

It had only been a dream, but Louisa should have held tighter to Mercy's hand. She should not have doubted her even for a moment.

"Darcelle! It's Louisa," she called from outside the tent.

The seamstress swept open the curtain of black, gold, and red and greeted her with a small smile. If possible, Darcelle's hair reached even higher, fancy braids spiraling on her head like a beautiful column and coiled tendrils framing her face. "I was just having breakfast. Why don't you join me?"

Louisa almost burst out her news then and there, but Darcelle turned, and Louisa had to dart past the curtain before it fell closed in her face. She followed Darcelle to the golden mound of fabrics where a tray of croissants rested alongside a bowl of fruit and cream. Darcelle smoothed her skirts as she sat.

"Where is Mercy?" Louisa peered around the tent's interior but saw no sign of her friend.

"She is elsewhere."

"With Fiona?"

"Sit, sit," Darcelle said instead of answering, a sure sign that Mercy was in big trouble for something she had not done.

Louisa removed her coat and scarf and lowered herself just above the cushions. She would have felt better had she seen Mercy, but her thoughts were so filled with hope for her father that she set aside her worry. Just for now. Everything would be cleared up soon enough.

Darcelle piled a plate with food, and Louisa accepted it, though it was more than she would be able to eat. Her belly was full with anticipation. "Thank you," she said, and was about to launch into her suspicions, but Darcelle spoke first.

"You seem to have taken to the carnival. I could not be more pleased."

Louisa fidgeted, impatient to speak.

"Your magic absolutely radiates." Darcelle's eyes glistened hungrily, and she sank her teeth into a croissant.

Louisa glanced down at herself but could not *see* her magic. Yet she knew it was there, despite the stolen bits. Maybe it was the hope, blooming and tending.

"You haven't tasted a thing," Darcelle said, stirring the cream and berries and lifting a spoonful to her mouth.

Louisa cupped her hand beneath her pastry, catching the crumbs that flaked off when she took a bite, and then set it back on the plate. Her words sat on her tongue, leaving no room for food. "I must tell you something."

Darcelle licked a drop of cream from the corner of her lip. "Yes?"

A gust of wind billowed the tent's curtain. Chimes tinkled and Louisa glanced up. The chandelier's red crystals seemed to have multiplied again, like magic. Perhaps Darcelle was replacing them one by one. It gladdened Louisa's heart—that broken things could be mended, that wrongs could be righted, and that lost things could be found.

Louisa touched her fingertips to her cheeks. "I think I have found my father." Speaking the words aloud made it seem even more real than holding the thoughts in her head.

Darcelle paused with her hand raised, a croissant almost to her lips. She looked at it with distaste, placed it back on the plate, and shoved it to the side. "Well, where is he, then?" Her eyes went wide with intense curiosity.

"I don't know. I mean, he's here. Somewhere. I just don't know where he is right this moment." Louisa shook her head. She wasn't making a bit of sense, so she stopped herself from saying anything about Mercy until she got her thoughts straightened out. One thing at a time. "I think Quiet Si is my father."

Louisa hoped to see the familiar thin-lipped smile spread across Darcelle's face, for her eyes to alight with surprise and gladness.

Darcelle's eyebrow twitched. "Well, most certainly this would be good tidings, only . . ." She set her hand atop Louisa's in a way people did when delivering bad news. Louisa tried to draw back, to put off hearing whatever Darcelle was about to say, but her words came forth. "It can't possibly be him."

"But it is! I know it!" Louisa burned as hot as Fire-Red Rosalyn's flames. She snatched her hand away, tucking it into her lap.

"You are mistaken. He is not your father," Darcelle said firmly, but not unkindly, leaving no room for argument. "For Quiet Si is a widower. He lost his wife long ago in a terrible accident that nearly killed him too. It took his eye, his leg, his jaw, and a good many fingers. I dare say, it took part of his heart and half his mind as well."

Louisa staggered to her feet, but Darcelle's words had already wormed their way into her head, casting doubt on what she'd moments before thought certain. "But . . ." Her sentence trailed off. Although she'd lined things up so neatly, the illusion distorted and her wishful hopes wilted.

Darcelle lowered her eyes and folded her hands, a pitying pose. "Louisa, my dear, my dear," she said, and then looked up through her lashes. "Have you never considered that your father is dead?"

⟆ 29 ⟆
A CLASH OF MAGIC

*D*ead.

Darcelle's words whipped through Louisa, shocking and horrible. She dropped to her knees just above the golden fabric. It was one thing to long for her father, imagining him out in the world somewhere, even if they were not together. It was quite another thing to think him dead, his last breaths already spent.

"No," Louisa choked out.

Darcelle pushed the dishes to the side and scooped Louisa closer, so her head rested in her lap. "There, there." She brushed Louisa's hair from her face, stroking the strands again and again. "You are no worse off now than you were moments before. You are where you belong. And where you are needed. With a new family who loves you."

"He isn't dead," Louisa whispered into Darcelle's soft

skirts, and just saying those words made her feel a little stronger. She turned her face upward. "I would know it if he were."

"You are so wishful," Darcelle said, patting Louisa's cheek. "But you must let the idea go, or it will eat up your heart."

"Like my mother." All those crunching love bugs devouring her insides and stealing her life away. Louisa pulled back from Darcelle's embrace, knocking against the dishes and spilling a splash of cream across the lovely fabric spread beneath them. She clasped one hand to her chest.

"How tragic and terrible," Darcelle said, dabbing at the tipped bowl of cream. "You do not want that fate for your own. Promise me you will move on."

Louisa would not end up like her mother. She'd fought against it from the start. But she did not want to make this promise either, not if she wasn't sure she could keep it. "I will do my best."

But even that wasn't true. If anything, she wanted to talk to Quiet Si more urgently. She had to know for certain.

"Your best is not good enough. You must be mindful of Quiet Si's heart. Do not speak to him of this, or you might well break it." Darcelle climbed to her feet and pulled Louisa up beside her. "Give me your promise."

Quiet Si must have been very fragile that he would need such fierce protecting. Louisa nodded. The last thing she wanted to do was hurt him. "I will be mindful."

"That is not the same thing as a promise."

Louisa drew back a step. "It is all I can give."

Darcelle coiled a strand of her lustrous hair around her finger. "Oh, you have *so* much to give, my dear."

Something moved at the periphery. Louisa glanced to the side, but there was nothing there, only the shelves of yarns and threads and ornamental costume flourishes. It must have been the light glinting off a jaw of rhinestones or a ribbon unraveling.

Or else it was Louisa's grief, tears brimming in her eyes.

She retrieved her coat and scarf but lingered at the tent's entrance, her thoughts too messy to properly express. "Thank you for breakfast," she said at last, though they were not the words in her heart, which screamed that her father was Quiet Si, but she knew Darcelle would never lie to her.

"Of course." Darcelle crossed to her worktable where fabric lay pinned and ready for cutting. She plucked a single piece of hair from her head and it darted through the needle she'd just raised. Darcelle lowered her voice. "And thank you for heeding me."

Louisa dipped her chin into the collar of her coat so Darcelle would not see the little frown settling on her lips and then backed out of the tent. She bumped into the wooden sign beside the entrance with Darcelle's name and title scripted in black, and a needle and thread painted on the other side.

Made by Quiet Si, like all the other boards.

Made by her *father*, who her mother had said sketched beneath the moon.

Except Darcelle said it was not possible.

What Louisa needed right then were her friends. All of them. They would listen to her ideas, no matter how farfetched they seemed.

She ran toward her tent, only to crash right into Ox and Jess as she took a sharp corner. "Ouch." Jess held her elbow.

Louisa rubbed her shin. "Where are you rushing to?" She glanced behind them, wondering if someone gave chase, but the pathway was empty.

"We're looking for you!" Jess straightened her knit hat, which had lowered over one eyebrow. "When I told Ox what you said about finding your misfortune, we thought you might be running off again."

"We wanted to stop you from going. I'm . . ." Ox flushed. "*We're* glad you're still here."

"I'm not going anywhere." This promise came swiftly, without anyone asking for it, and it was one she knew she could keep. "There is too much to do." And though she still had to untangle her thoughts about Quiet Si, finding the source of the darkness within the carnival was more urgent.

Ox's golden eyes flashed. "We have to snare the butterfly." He smacked his hands together, and then cupped them, as if he'd trapped something between his palms.

"But if the thief's not Fiona, who is it?" Jess asked.

Footsteps approached from behind, and voices drifted closer, whispers about the carnival's dark troubles. It was all anyone could talk about.

Louisa held a finger to her lips and led Ox and Jess past the tents and into the Spark Woods. They tucked themselves away from everyone else just as they had the first time they'd plotted, settling on the leaf-strewn ground under the maples' bowed branches.

But without Mercy beside them, their circle did not feel complete.

Jess must have felt the same, for she looked at the empty space and said, "I wish Mercy were here."

"It is up to us to clear her name, and then she will be back beside us," Louisa said, sounding more confident than she felt.

"But even Mercy thinks her shadows might be misbehaving." A sharp ache broke Jess's voice.

"Yes, but if the shadows are disobedient that does not mean Mercy is to blame." And if that was true, Louisa thought, maybe what Darcelle had said was also true—that it *was only some strange clash of magic.* "What if Mercy's magic collided with someone else's?"

Her shadows might have masked the true culprit. They might have tried to *deflect* the magic (which could explain why her hair had not silvered), but the magic had slipped through the carnival, hungrily stealing more and more.

"What do we know for sure?" Jess asked.

Ox held out his hand and touched one index finger to another, counting off each item. "Firstly, that creepy storm blew through, and secondly, a shadow sneaked out and pulled Raven from the rope."

"Thirdly"—Jess leaned forward, eager to contribute—"shadows meddled with Mina's magic and Lovely Valentine's too."

"Something *like* a shadow," Louisa said. "It was not the same."

"What did it feel like?" Ox said, who had so far escaped the magic's attentions.

"My skin was all pins and needles." Louisa shuddered at the memory. "And then . . . it felt as if a part of me was snipped away." A hole had been carved into her very core, one she worried might never heal.

"It has to be someone with magic," Jess said. "How else could they take it? How else would they know how to use it?"

"What's the good of little scraps of magic?" Ox, who had an abundance of magic, asked. "How would that do anyone any good?"

"I wish I had even a teaspoon of magic." Jess frowned. "Maybe the scraps can be patched together into something bigger." Hope gleamed in her eye, as if, Louisa thought, the magic might be made into a cloak and wrapped around Jess's shoulders, granting her access to a magic she'd never otherwise know.

Or maybe the scraps could create something even larger than a cloak.

"Like the fence surrounding the carnival," Louisa said. The wooden beams and barbed wire hummed with magic. Just a touch. Just enough to keep trespassers out and the carnival safe from anything prowling within the woods. Louisa tried to remember the way Fiona had described it. "Isn't the carnival itself wrapped with the fabric of magic?" And there was so much more. "Magic is everywhere around us. What about the silver threads tying the sky basket to the moon and tethering the magical butterflies to the boat? After the storm, maybe the whole carnival was in need of some patching."

"I thought we were talking about thieving. All this talk of fabric, and needles and threads, and snipping and patching. We aren't sewing magic, are we?" Ox grumbled.

Louisa froze.

"Yes." She latched on to Ox's last comment, trying to hold of the idea that seemed ready to fly out of her head. "That's it."

Ox's smile went wide. "It is?" For once he did not say that he wished he'd thought of the idea, because this time, he *had* come up with it (even if he didn't seem to realize the whole of it quite yet).

All Louisa could think of was how much they'd missed, how much they'd been deceived. She had let warm arms console her, had listened as a low voice told her she was needed—that her magic radiated. And that she had so much to give. "Jess, let me see your hands."

Jess held them out. The tiny silver scars looked like the most delicate embroidery. "Who healed your cuts?"

"Darcelle."

But this Louisa already knew. "Who tends the threads for Moon Rides?"

"Darcelle," said Ox.

"Who tends the threads for Butterfly Boat Rides?"

"Darcelle," said Jess.

"But I thought she was a marvel with a wondrous talent for sewing and nothing more? That she had no magic?" Even as Louisa said it, she knew she'd been mistaken. Those fine silver threads, just like the long, long threads of hair Darcelle had woven into Louisa's scarf, linked everything together. Hadn't Louisa just seen one of those hairs thread *itself* through Darcelle's needle?

Hadn't Darcelle given Louisa the silver thread that sent her kite soaring into the air without need of wind?

"Oh, she's a marvel all right, but she's got plenty of magic too," Jess said.

"More than anyone," Ox agreed.

Louisa's heart thumped. Though it was too early for the moon's appearance, she looked up, as if she might find it in the sky. It wasn't there, of course, but her eyes fixed on a spot of gold in the distance—the kite she'd made as a stepping-stone for her father.

You have a star catcher, Quiet Si had said.

Louisa trembled, thinking of the words she'd read earlier that morning. *For the star who brightens my life.* Her mother was his star, and they'd first met that long-ago day when he'd been flying the kite. It *had* caught him a star.

All her doubts fell away. She *knew* her father.

Darcelle had lied about everything.

Louisa had overlooked every warning, even ones stated so obviously. The leotard Darcelle started sewing for Louisa *before* Raven had fallen, as if the seamstress knew what was to come because she had planned it.

And other things too.

"The day I tried to leave the carnival, the sinister storm blew through. Darcelle was the one who directed me to Northrup. And she told me that she'd see me again. What if she made it so? Those dark threads reaching out after me, they must have been hers, somehow tangled up in Mercy's shadows."

Louisa gulped. What if those same silver threads had interfered with others before her?

No wonder no one had ever left the carnival. Darcelle Duval would not let them go.

⤾30↲
ELSEWHERE

Louisa sat silent and wide-eyed, waiting for Ox and Jess to say something. The cold slipped through her coat, and she shivered. For all she knew, Darcelle could reach them here in the woods, tossing out silver threads from her endless pile of hair and tying knots around their ankles as she dragged them back to her.

"Darcelle tricked you." Jess turned from Louisa to Ox, balling her hands into tight fists. "She tricked all of us."

It didn't matter that they had nowhere else to go. They couldn't leave even if they wanted to. Darcelle would always be ready to grab hold and tug them back.

Louisa thought of the very first day she'd met the seamstress, how she'd believed Darcelle might have stitched the carnival into being. "She's the Seamstress of the Carnival and tugs all the threads. She's sewn us all so close she mustn't think our magic is separate from her own. She must feel she's *entitled* to it."

Leaves swirled up from the ground and then scattered, disrupted by Ox's temper. Branches swayed and creaked, but he clamped down on his magic before it let loose. "It isn't right. Our magic isn't hers to take."

"Of course it's not," Louisa said, and though it upset her, she breathed a sigh of relief that they believed her—and that they had finally found the answer they'd sought for so long. But there was still so much ahead, and it seemed daunting, for how could they stop someone so powerful? "Darcelle will only take more. That must be why she swept Mercy away—to steal all her magic for good. To keep it from wrestling her own."

Jess's eyes darkened. "And because she needs someone to blame for the mess she's made."

"Darcelle will never release Mercy," Louisa whispered. It was too horrible to consider. That they might never see their friend again.

"We've got to stop her." Ox jumped to his feet, as if he meant to run off right then without thought or plan, led only by his heart, which he left unguarded in a way Louisa thought she'd never be able to match.

"What can *we* do?" Jess plucked a leaf from the sleeve of her coat and frowned at it mournfully. She looked so unlike herself. Her smile had dimmed, her shoulders rounded—

the way she caved in on herself whenever she thought about her lack of magic.

But Louisa saw all the special things within her friend that Jess could not. And within Ox too. They were more than a playful, magicless girl and a skinny boy without a father. In their hearts, one was a goblin, the other a beast. And Louisa, she was more than a motherless girl whose feet never touched the ground; she was a starlark.

With these thoughts held close, Louisa stood and pulled Jess up beside her. "First, we must steal back Mercy." Louisa drew in a deep breath, floating a little higher into the air. It felt good, as if she were taking back what Darcelle had snatched away. "Then we must expose Darcelle." And lastly, she would talk to Quiet Si, but she kept that thought to herself. It was something she had to do alone.

Jess's face brightened, ready to be snapped from her gray mood.

"But where is Mercy?" Ox asked.

"Darcelle said she is *elsewhere*." It was the same phrasing Quiet Si had used when Louisa asked where the magical butterflies had gone. She'd thought it a meaningless phrase, but maybe it was a real place. Somewhere hidden.

"That's not helpful," Ox said.

"It is too. If Mercy is *elsewhere*, at least we know she's not *here*." Jess looked around.

Louisa pictured Quiet Si the day she'd found him by

the pond, trying to remember which way he'd gazed off when referring to elsewhere, hoping to at least have some direction from which to start. "Westward." Louisa pointed toward the Spark Woods. "I think."

If Louisa and her friends moved more deeply into the trees, if they lost sight of the carnival, they might not find their way back to it.

But it was a risk Louisa knew they had to take.

Jess looped one arm with Ox, the other with Louisa, and together, they strode forward. They did not speak as they prowled the woods, not even Jess; they were too intent on listening and watching for any sign of Mercy or Darcelle.

The carnival fell farther and farther behind them until Louisa could no longer see even the faintest outline. And the woods grew darker and darker as the clouds thickened and morning passed to afternoon. None of them complained of being tired or hungry. None of them raised their fears of being lost. But Louisa worried she had led them astray.

"I think we passed by here before," Ox said, stopping suddenly. He pointed at a lightning-struck tree, blackened and broken and unmistakable.

"I think you are right," Louisa admitted.

Jess stepped away from them and opened her mouth wide. "Mercy!" She turned around and called again. "Mercy!" Neither Louisa nor Ox quieted her, for they were so far from the carnival surely no one at all could hear them. Her voiced echoed through the trees and then drifted away.

Mercy did not answer, and Louisa didn't want to think that it was because she *couldn't*. Maybe she just hadn't heard Jess's call.

"Mercy would be able to find us if we went missing. She'd send one of her messengers and quick as that"—Ox snapped his fingers—"it would drag us to her."

Louisa swung her head toward Ox. Her hands flew to her mouth. "Oh my goodness." For weeks and weeks, she had carried around the shadow Mercy had gifted her. *In case you need it,* Mercy had said. There was no better time to use it than now.

Louisa reached into her pocket, searching. Her mother's little pair of scissors poked her thumb, and she fumbled past them, fingertips closing around the smallest slip of a shadow.

Ox and Jess moved closer, looking at her expectantly. She withdrew her hand and held it out between them. Slowly, she uncurled her fingers. The patch of darkness shifted and rippled like impenetrable fog, as if Mercy had instructed it to await its orders.

Ox grinned. Jess leaned forward. She poked the shadow.

"Go on," Louisa said. "I don't know how to use it any better than you do."

Without hesitation, Jess snatched the smoky shadow. Her face grayed, the shadow casting darkness the way a candle cast soft light. "It weighs nothing, but it feels like everything." She cupped it in her palm, this fragile piece of magic she'd never held before.

And now she would command it.

"Travel true." Jess raised her arm and then threw the shadow into the air in the same manner as Mercy—with all her might. "Fetch Mercy."

The shadow launched into the sky, arcing swift and sure. Somehow, Mercy had crafted it to listen to a different voice than her own, and it had waited, patiently, for this very moment.

"Follow it," Ox said, charging away, with Jess fast on his heels.

Eyes turned skyward, Louisa chased the shadow and her friends. They wove in and out of the maples. Their breaths came loud and labored. In the distance, a black-and-gold tent rose above the treetops. They'd circled back toward the carnival.

Louisa should have known they would. Darcelle would never stray far from it—or let Mercy leave it.

The shadow looped through the air and then dived. It blended with all the other shades of gray, seamlessly seeping back into the darkest corners. Ox and Jess stumbled to a stop, and Louisa floated beside them, breathing hardest of them all, still weakened from her loss of magic.

They stood in a small clearing. Ash coated the ground instead of fallen leaves, and the trees around them stretched tall, brittle, and dead, branches spiked like lances, trunks spiraled with silver webs. It looked more like Plum, a polluted place, than the Spark Woods.

"Where is she?" Jess whispered.

Wings flapped, and Louisa looked to the sky. There were dark clouds aplenty, but not a single bird overhead. The feather-like rustling came louder.

"What was that?" Ox snarled, incisors bared.

Louisa sneaked forward, her feet quiet as ever, listening to the woods. All was silent.

Ahead, blackened branches pushed up from the earth. They crossed one another at sharp angles, the strangest sort of cage, and within them, something stirred.

Another flutter of movement. Shuffling. A hushed sigh.

"Mercy?" Louisa crept closer and closer.

Blurred motion, a flash of gold and a whisper of black. So many wings, flapping and flapping. The magic-born butterflies swarmed together and apart, trapped in the briar and branches.

Louisa ran toward the thorny cage. She curled her hands around the twigs. The butterflies, large as bats, pressed to get nearer to where she stood. Their long, thin tongues unfurled, as if they thought she'd brought nectar. Or maybe they drank magic.

But she had nothing to offer them.

As much as she hated to see them confined in this manner, Mercy needed her more than they did, and Louisa turned away, eyes sweeping the ash-covered ground and the twisted trees and the oversized spiderwebs draped from the branches.

Louisa inched closer to the nearest maple. Something about the silver-strung webbing struck her as both frightful and beautiful.

And familiar.

"Ox," she whispered. "Jess." They hurried from the cage of butterflies to her side.

Louisa reached out, hesitantly, her hand brushing the filament. It neither stuck to her fingertips nor tore at her touch. In fact, it wasn't webbing at all but a strange sort of thread, cold as could be and so carefully stitched. Something this masterful could only have been made by Darcelle's careful hand.

Her *magical* hand.

Louisa tugged the thread. At first, it resisted, but then she unraveled the thinnest strand. It must have curled around the trunk a thousand times. She pulled it as she slipped forward, circling to the other side of the tree with Ox and Jess.

All at once, they froze.

A slim figure was caught within the silver threads. A pale brown face. Arms and legs and a tangle of hair.

Against the black-barked tree slumped Fiona Dior.

⚬ 31 ⚬
COBWEBS & LACE

Fiona's head drooped on her chest. Her blue-tinged eyelids rested closed. On the ground by her feet, roses and violets, daisies and poppies that should have been the color of sunshine, lay in all manner of decay. The last blush of pink faded from a peony and then crumbled to ash.

A graveyard of flowers and magic lay beneath their feet.

And Fiona slouched before them, hair limp on her shoulders, all of it gone silver.

She must have crossed Darcelle, mindless of her own misfortune, hoping to help Mercy above all else.

There was no sign of Mercy or Darcelle.

Louisa trembled, dropping the silver thread. It crawled back toward its tree, as if it had memories and knew where to return. She watched it apprehensively. It slithered, so well behaved, following the magical orders Darcelle must have used to charm it.

Ox reached toward the threads. They reached back, lashing like a whip around his finger. He winced, tearing loose before they could grasp him more firmly, and stuffed his hands into his coat pockets. All of them took a step back.

Never once did Fiona move.

"Is she dead?" Jess's eyes reddened, as if she might burst into tears.

"Of course not," Ox said, fierce and protective. "She's just . . . magicked."

Louisa was not sure of anything. Fiona held so still and made not a sound. "Fiona?"

They waited a breath and then another. From across the small clearing came the soft beating of butterfly wings, like a too-fast pulse.

Suddenly, Fiona's eyes rolled behind her lids.

"Did you see? Did you see?" Jess exclaimed.

"I told you she wasn't dead." Ox's breath shuddered out in relief.

"Fiona," Louisa repeated, waiting for Fiona to open her eyes, to tell them what they should do. How they could defeat Darcelle and save Mercy. They needed her.

But the misfortune teller did not stir again.

"We've got to free her." Swallowing her fear, Louisa tore at the magical strands. Darcelle could return at any moment. She could trap them all.

Ox and Jess leaped forward, plucking at the knots and

dancing away whenever a strand took a swipe at them. They tore and tugged, ruining all the stitching.

The threads fought against their meddling. They slunk away from groping fingers, only to snug more tightly against Fiona, wrapping around her ankles and wrists and neck, securing her firmly to the tree.

"They won't let her go." Jess swatted at a lone thread curling sneakily closer, dodging away before it could wrap around her elbow.

"What if they've got hold of Mercy too?" Louisa did not want to leave Fiona there, caught so helplessly in the threads, but she turned away, scanning the woods.

"We'll find her." Ox bounded off, purposeful, as if he had no doubt she could be found.

"Quietly." Louisa cringed at the crunch of Ox's boots on the leaves. Her eyes scraped the trees, looking not for Mercy this time—but for Darcelle.

The seamstress might have already been in the woods.

Louisa floated in the opposite direction Ox had gone to search for Mercy. The pair circled round the trees at the edge of the clearing, searching each silver-threaded trunk. Every dead tree looked haunted. Weeks or months or years ago, Darcelle must have trapped other poor souls here, their very magic drained, blood and bones sapped of what made them special. All so she could have it for herself.

Louisa glanced behind her.

No ghosts followed.

The only one there was Jess, resolutely plucking at the threads, even as they curled around her, more aggressive now that the three of them were not together. "Get off," she demanded as they lashed out, wriggling and sneaking and tightening their hold.

Trusting that Jess could keep them at bay, Louisa faced forward again. Nearer and nearer, she and Ox came toward each other, Mercy nowhere to be found. When they completed the circle, he lifted his head, meeting Louisa's eyes. Goose bumps shivered across her skin. It was not the cold (though she felt it deep inside) but the stricken look on his face that chilled her.

He shook his head. "Where is she?"

"She must be here." Louisa would not give up, and she would not let the doubt wiggle into Ox's thoughts either. "Can't you . . . Oh, I don't know. Can't you reach for her the way you lift a stone from the ground?"

She did not understand his magic, not exactly. But she hoped it could help them.

Ox's eyes blazed gold. "If she's near. Maybe. I'm better at lifting things when I see them." On the ground, the ash stirred. Above them, the branches swayed. "But maybe . . ."

Louisa's heart skipped. She followed Ox as he stumbled backward a few paces, and then a few paces more, before stopping in front of a black-barked maple, wider than any other around them. Threads hung flimsily from the branches.

And almost hidden against the gnarled trunk crouched a shaded hollow.

"Ox? Louisa?" Jess said.

But Louisa hardly heard her. She was too focused on the tree before her and the strange patchwork of threads twisting up from the ground. Silver and black tangled together, stretching like cobwebs and lace across a dark gash in the bark.

She could not tell how deep the scar ran.

She leaned closer.

And closer still.

Fingers snaked fast between the threads.

Louisa reeled back, colliding with Ox. The fingers shrank away.

Ox wiped a hand across his dampened brow, and his words came winded. "I tried to pull her free."

"Oh no, Mercy can't be stuck in there." Louisa dropped to her knees just above the ground, plunging her hand into the threads and webs.

"Louisa! Ox!"

Jess's strangled voice echoed through the woods. Louisa jerked her head to the side, shaken through and through. Even at a distance she could see the threads writhing around Jess. Like night smothering day, they scrambled around her, binding her limb by limb to the tree. Whip-fast, they covered her mouth.

Silencing her.

"Get back!" Ox pulled Louisa's arm, but it was too late. The same dark threads that masked the tree's hollow leaped forward, twining around her waist and dragging her forward with incredible strength.

Ox stood very still, a look of concentration on his face, but the force of the threads' magic must have been too powerful for him to control with his mind. They neither slowed nor stopped their attack.

Louisa tried to float up into the air, but the threads kept hold, locking onto her arm, ensnaring her. Ox scrambled in the underbrush, grasping hold of a crooked stick. He swung at the threads but only managed to tangle the branch within them.

Jess had asked what sort of magic this was. And of course, it was Darcelle's strange needlework. Dark magic stitched into every strand.

They needed something sharper than a stick to cut through. Something made to snip thread, magical or otherwise.

They needed a mighty weapon—a knife or a sword.

Or *scissors*!

One handed, Louisa fumbled in her pocket. And there, right where she'd left them, was her mother's little pair of sewing shears. She slipped her fingers into the finger holes and lashed out, cutting the threads as fast as she could.

They recoiled, falling away from her wrist and her waist.

She snipped and slashed. "Ox!" she cried.

He was already beside her, focused intently on the hollow, or rather, what was inside it. The threads quivered.

A hand pressed against the stitching, stretching it outward. It looked frightful. A creature emerging from darkness.

Louisa kept snipping, again and again, until she unveiled the whole of the hollow. With what must have been a great tug of his mind, Ox yanked.

A small body flopped forth from the tree, landing facefirst in the ash. Shadows swarmed the figure head to toe, armor against Darcelle's dark magic. As the autumn wind blew through, the shadows loosened their hold.

A gasp issued forth.

"Mercy!" Louisa bent toward her friend, brushing a strand of brown hair from her cheek.

Mercy grunted.

Warily, Ox eyed the narrow crevice in the tree. The threads hung lifeless, but there was no telling if they retained any magic or if the scissors had stripped them of power. Without moving a muscle, he lifted Mercy, letting the air carry her out of the clearing and into the leaf-strewn woods. "Help Jess."

Louisa cast one last, long look at Mercy and then darted toward Jess, who struggled furiously against the threads. But for all her thrashing, they did not let her go.

"Hold still," Louisa said, and when still Jess wriggled, Louisa bit her lip, lifted the scissors, and clipped the gleaming threads, hoping she would not cut Jess in the process.

The threads uncoiled from Jess's mouth. "Get them off! Get them off!"

Louisa snipped again and again, until Jess broke free, and Fiona too, who slid to the ground in a heap.

Jess swung Louisa into a hug. Their hearts pounded against each other.

They were safe. Everyone would be okay.

And then they were torn apart.

SKYBORNE

Cold whistled through Louisa as she lost her hold on Jess. They both cried out. Their fingers touched one last time.

Jess fell backward, landing with a thud. Louisa flew into the air, pulled up, up, up by the scarf wrapped twice around her neck. The beautiful red scarf Darcelle had gifted her.

The one she should have torn from her neck the moment she'd realized Darcelle's dark intentions. After all, those long tinseled threads of Darcelle's hair wound through it.

It lifted her, infused with magic all this time, and there was nothing Louisa could do about it. She clutched the scarf with one hand, keeping it from tightening around her neck. With her other hand, she gripped the scissors. Her legs flailed. She drifted farther and farther from the ground, from Ox at the edge of the woods with Mercy, from Jess by the tree with Fiona . . .

. . . and from Darcelle Duval.

The seamstress swept into the clearing, her mouth twisted in anger. Her cheeks matched her scarlet skirts, and as she whirled about, casting her eyes at the threads' destruction, she stirred up ash, spotting her hem gray. Stacked high atop her head, her lovely hair flamed the brightest red, as if it had sucked all the color from the dead ring of maples. As if it had sucked all the magic it could from the world.

She shrieked, a horrible cry, like a raven shot through the heart with an arrow. The sound carried sharply, all the way to Louisa, who now floated as high as the treetops. She could see the carnival in the distance.

Somehow, Darcelle had known what she, Jess, and Ox were up to.

"Look what you've done," Darcelle hissed. She caressed the silver threads trailing from the branches of the nearest tree. They were drawn to her touch, shifting closer, as if a breeze blew them toward her. Slowly, they entwined. They *mended*. It was an amazing sight, such a delicate magic, except that Louisa knew just what terrible things those threads could do.

"Look what *you've* done." Jess swiped her hair out of her face, marking her cheek with a smudge of ash.

Darcelle's head whipped to the side. Step by step, she crept toward Jess, who climbed unsteadily to her feet.

Louisa gasped for air, trying to loosen the scarf. It clung to her like a snake hoping to squeeze out her life. "Run." The word croaked out of her throat.

Jess only planted her feet more firmly and cinched her brows together stubbornly. "Leave us alone."

Darcelle lifted her jaw.

"Or . . ." Jess mirrored the seamstress's pose and thrust out her chin.

Darcelle stalked closer, kicking up ash.

"Or . . ." Jess's voice wavered, but she held her ground. "We will destroy you."

A brittle laugh crawled up Darcelle's throat. Her tower of hair tilted back at an impossible angle, each strand glinting and writhing, as if it might come undone and raze the night. "For such a useless, magicless girl, you have too bold a tongue."

Heat flared within Louisa, and she wrestled with the scarf, which closed like an iron vise around her throat. She struggled hopelessly, forced to watch as her friend faced Darcelle alone.

The newly repaired threads spiraled around Darcelle's fingers, and then she thrust out her hands and launched them forward. They darted around Jess's wrists and ankles, cinching tighter and tighter.

Jess tottered a moment and then fell.

Louisa stared in horror as her friend went limp. She had to find a way to the ground. She had to stop Darcelle before it was too late. Raising the scissors, Louisa hacked at the scarf.

Darcelle's head swiveled upward. Her features twisted. "Cut my threads and they will cut into you."

Pins and needles pierced Louisa's core. The scarf's tinseled threads of hair slashed at her magic.

Ox darted into the clearing. He seemed to *throw* his magic outward, as all at once Darcelle stumbled. The toes of her slippers lifted off the ground.

And then she set down again. Darcelle raged with magic, too much for Ox to manage. He staggered backward, catching himself against a blackened tree trunk.

Darcelle tore her eyes away from Louisa, sending ribbons of silver around Ox. They coiled through the air and wrapped around his eyes. He wedged his fingers under the threads, but they remained snug on his face, lengthening and coiling the length of his body, until he tripped, falling hard to the ground.

The scarf dug into Louisa's windpipe. She could hardly breathe. Dark spots danced at the corners of her vision. All she could think of were Ox's words: *I'm better at lifting things when I see them.* And Darcelle had blocked his sight.

Louisa could not pass out. Could not give up. Caught

in the air, she braced herself against the pins-and-needles magic digging into her and snipped the scarf.

Darcelle flinched with each cut of the yarn.

As if it pained her.

She must have felt Louisa snipping away at her magic when they released Mercy from the hollow. That's how she knew they were here.

Louisa made one final cut. The scarf fell away from her neck, faster than she expected.

The scissors snagged in the yarn, slipping from her hand and tumbling the long way down to the ground. They stabbed the earth and the hem of Darcelle's dress. She glared up at Louisa, but then a thin smile sliced across her face. "Floating there so helplessly, you remind me exactly of Quiet Si"—Darcelle's voice sank into Louisa like teeth and nails—"the day I yanked him from the sky."

Louisa filled with dread. "No!" Her voice rattled the treetops, echoing through the clearing. It was everything she'd feared, and also everything she'd hoped for, and she did not know how to untangle her emotions—or her limbs. She floundered in the air, just as Mercy had teased her for doing, but no matter how she flailed, she came no closer to the earth. "We trusted you."

That was the sharpest blow of all. How welcome Louisa had felt, how cared for and accepted. And Darcelle had only wanted their magic.

"Why?" Louisa's question vibrated shrilly from her throat. She could not understand it, how someone could be so awful.

"Why not? When I am thirsty, I drink." Darcelle straightened the sleeves of her dress. "And you all hold an endless well of magic to sip from."

Louisa's mouth went dry. "You are filled with greed."

"Is it greedy to take what is mine? I am the Seamstress of the Carnival. I stitched it to life when it was weak. It, and everything—every*one*—inside it, belongs to me. Your magic is payment. It is owed to me."

"But you are hurting us all. You could have killed Quiet Si." And Louisa feared that she and her friends would be next, now that they knew Darcelle's secret. She exhaled all the air from her lungs but lowered only an inch. Not nearly enough. Even that small effort left her winded, her magic in tatters, its hum a jagged pulse inside her.

"Oh, I didn't mean to tug him so fiercely. He broke apart. Bones are fragile things, you know. So are hearts. I warned you of that, didn't I?"

Louisa had thought herself selfish for wanting to find her father above all else, but facing down Darcelle, she saw how different they were from each other. Lonesomeness and love had driven Louisa, and Darcelle (though perhaps just as lonely as Louisa had been) had love for no one other than herself.

With a swift jerk of her skirts, Darcelle tore the material free from the scissors. She pressed her fingers together, and, as if she held a needle between them, she knit up the tear in the fabric with no more than two swishes of her wrist.

Far above, Louisa watched helplessly as Darcelle spun round, her eyes searching the woods and landing on Mercy. Mercy had not yet lifted her head. She lay there, vulnerable, without her shadows to protect her.

Louisa let out another breath, willing herself lower in the sky. But even after all these weeks, she still had not perfected her descent and remained where she was, skyborne.

But she could not let the wind or Darcelle or anything else, especially her fear, control her. This magic was her own, and if she wanted to keep Darcelle from stealing more of it away, she had to master it.

Louisa did not want to end up like her brokenhearted mother, watching as her friends lost their magic, and she did not want to end up like her father either, without his yesterdays or his name.

Quiet Si.

Oh, she wished he were here. He'd known what she needed to do, the memory of his mystique buried deep inside him without recognizing it for what it was. He'd told her how to control her movement, and she thought of his words now, let them wash over her, as if he were there beside her.

Close your eyes.

Louisa shut her lids. The snarl on Darcelle's lips was the last thing she saw.

Take a step.

Louisa swept her leg forward.

Just one step.

Letting out a breath, she set her foot down, imagining a stairway winding all the way to the ground. A second step followed the first. On the third, she squinted open her eyes.

Her heart sank.

She'd come no closer to the ground.

⚬ **33** ⚬
THE FOREST OF STARS

Louisa had no time to waste.

"Ox, help," she hissed, hoping the sound of her voice would allow him to find her, to latch on to her. He made no reply, but his head cocked in her direction. "Ox!"

His invisible touch brushed against and then past her. Louisa swung her arms through the air, as if she could snatch hold of his fleeting magic.

Darcelle Duval crept closer and closer to Mercy, never once glancing back. She must have thought Louisa posed no threat at all—that she would remain stuck in the sky until Darcelle was ready to deal with her.

"Shadow Spinner," Darcelle muttered. "Always interfering. Like water and oil. Shadow and thread."

Louisa quaked.

Below, Ox's body lurched. A sudden heaviness coursed through Louisa, a great weight in all her limbs. With Darcelle distracted, she plummeted through the air, *fast, fast, fast,* a jerky descent that left her head spinning, even after Ox's magic released her. The slightest breeze might blow her away again.

One eye on Darcelle, one eye on the ground, Louisa searched for the scissors. They'd flown through the air when Darcelle pulled her skirt free, and Louisa had not seen where they landed.

She had to hurry, before Darcelle stuffed Mercy back into the tree, cocooning her in magic too strong to break. For after, Darcelle would bind the rest of them to the tree trunks, stealing their magic until none remained.

But no, Darcelle had said they had an endless well within them. Perhaps the way hope lingered, even when Louisa thought it gone for good. She held both close, magic and hope, determined that Darcelle would steal neither.

Louisa inched forward, gaze focused on the ground. And there, a glint of silver in the ash. Not the threads but the scissors.

She leaped toward them.

Sneaking from behind the tree trunk, long fingers closed around the blades.

Louisa nearly cried out but clapped a hand to her mouth, smothering the sound.

And her small smile.

Fiona leaned around the tree. She tried to stand but crumpled again, legs giving out. "Take them," she whispered, and lifted a weak arm, holding out the scissors.

Their eyes met, their fingers touched. Fiona raised her other hand to her hair, always seeking misfortunes. A single daisy, small and faded, bloomed from the silver strands. Louisa waited a tremulous moment, expecting Fiona to tell her more, to tell her what to do, but maybe the future was not yet determined (or maybe it was too horrible to voice), for she said nothing.

Clutching the scissors, Louisa turned away from Fiona. She would forge her own future, the one her heart showed her, instead of waiting for it to unfold.

Fast-footed, she ran to Ox and Jess, who grumbled and tossed on the ground, wound up in the threads. The moment she cut them free, Darcelle would know. She'd *feel* it.

But it could not be helped.

Louisa snipped swiftly, breaking the bindings and Ox's blindfold. Ox and Jess shook off the threads, as if their skin crawled with grubs and worms. They stood side by side by side as Darcelle shrieked and turned to face them.

Louisa trembled. How small the scissors seemed in her hand.

"I've had enough of you!" Spittle flew from between Darcelle's red lips. This time, she did not look at Mercy but at Louisa. The seamstress jabbed her finger forward, so forcefully Louisa took a step back, though Darcelle had not touched her. "Ruining my lovely threads, poking at Si's memories. He's started to resist my magic, when always before I took it without his notice."

As Mercy had wondered, it did all begin when Louisa arrived, but Darcelle was the only one at fault.

"Then why did you not let me go? You sent the storm of threads. You forced me to return." Louisa held the scissors high, hoping Darcelle did not seeing the shaking of her hand. "Why not let Mercy go when her magic clashed with your own?"

"So someone else might take your magic? So you might hoard it selfishly? Oh no." Darcelle let out a grating laugh. "Remember, you all belong to me."

"We don't," said Ox.

"Nope," said Jess.

"Never," said Louisa.

"Oh, but you are mistaken. There is no better way to master someone than to allow them to think they have their own will. Do you think you arrived here by chance or fortune? By some choice of your own?"

Louisa *had* chosen to come, yet without the invitation, she never would have. Her heart and her thoughts sped away from her. Fiona must have thought the invitations offered a kindness, but all along Darcelle had been pulling the strings. Luring Louisa and her friends.

Luring Louisa's father!

"You left an invitation for my father. You invited him to stay, and when he refused, you snatched him back."

"And then I waited, all these years and ever so patiently . . . for you. But no more!" With a flash of her hands, Darcelle called the silver threads from every tree limb, from every branch and hollow. They writhed into a frenzy.

And then they dived. In a swarm of magic, they slithered toward Louisa and her friends. This time, they would neither bind nor restrain—they would take what they wanted.

Louisa stepped forward; she wielded the scissors like a sword.

Behind Darcelle, leaves rustled. Mercy groggily pushed herself up on her forearms. She tilted back her head, caught in Darcelle's long shadow.

Louisa knew it was all Mercy needed.

Mercy plucked the shadow right from the air and sent it racing. It swooped over Darcelle's head, colliding with the silver threads just before they crashed into Louisa.

"No!" Darcelle raked her nails down her cheeks. She swiveled on her heel, and her arm lashed out, snatching for Mercy.

Louisa ran forward. Ox's and Jess's feet pounded behind her. The dark threads twined around them like the sharpest pins and needles. But Louisa did not slow. She slashed and snipped, shearing through the threads again and again, even as they tried to twist away.

Darcelle shrieked with each cut, as if the blades sliced skin instead of thread. Lustrous strands slipped loose from her tower of hair. They clasped hold of Mercy, who still seemed so weak, and dragged her toward the tree. The dark hollow gaped, ready to swallow her.

Jess rushed ahead, through the churning mass around them. It seemed hardly to touch her, for she had no magic to take. She lunged for Darcelle's ankles. Jess and the seamstress toppled to the ground.

Darcelle's hair tore and recoiled, releasing Mercy, and Ox must have lifted Darcelle, for she swung up from the ground and into the sky. Her skirts flapped in the wind.

Louisa had only moments before Darcelle would bear down on them with her wrath. Louisa sucked in a breath and spun into the air despite her worries that the wind would never let her down again.

Silver threads crackled like lightning. Darcelle's eyes burned with fury, focused intently on Louisa. "I will break you, as I broke your father. You will be my toy, my plaything. A marionette, trapped forever to the ground. And your magic will feed the carnival. It will be mine."

"You can't have it." Louisa rose as high as Darcelle. The wind knocked them back and forth, shadows twisting around them now that Mercy had awakened.

"Oh, but I can." Darcelle stitched magic in the palm of

her hand, glimmering threads, and then sent them flying. They sizzled straight for Louisa.

Louisa flung herself to the side, out of their immediate reach, but they angled back toward her. Darcelle started to drop in the air, as if Ox had let her go, but she directed threads to each wrist and to the nearest tree branches. They slowed her descent, lowering her gently.

Head down, arm held forward, Louisa soared through the air after Darcelle. Sharp pinpricks jabbed at her skin, stabbing right through her coat. Threads tangled around her body, clustering so close to her face, whipping so fast past her eyes, she could see nothing beyond them. Not the sky. Not the ground.

Not Darcelle.

Louisa felt herself drifting higher, but not of her own doing. It was her magic weakening. Darcelle thieving. Silver shot up the strands of Louisa's hair. The forest of stars—so vast, so lovely and frightful—reached for her, closer than it had ever been before.

Wind chimes tinkled, an unlovely sound. They rang like a funeral bell, like a death knell. The oversweet clinking of Darcelle's chandelier, each red crystal like a tick mark of the magic she'd stolen.

Darcelle gathered the threads again. No matter how long Louisa fought them off, they would mend, they would take *more*.

Louisa had to stop her. She had to take back what had been stolen.

Storm clouds churned. So high above, Louisa's hair tousled in her face and she swatted at the silver tips.

Silver-tipped hair.

And Darcelle's hair so very, very vibrant, so very, very willful.

If hair lost color when magic was stolen, then perhaps the opposite held true as well. Perhaps Darcelle's silken hair coursed with all her magic.

Louisa clicked open and closed the scissors just as Darcelle sent an angry spiral of thread skyward. A burst of hope shot through Louisa. She fought with renewed energy, shredding ribbons of silver and sending them to the ground.

Which she still could not reach on her own.

Which she *had* to reach on her own.

This time Louisa did not close her eyes. She faced her fears, looking first to the Spark Woods far below and then to the forest of stars so wide above.

She would not be smashed to the ground or blown away. She would soar where she wanted, chasing the golden soot of those stars and then passing it by. Led by nothing other than her will, her heart, her magic. It hummed inside her.

She had only to listen to it.

Louisa took one step after another downward, faster this time, until she hovered right above Darcelle's tower of hair. Unflinchingly, she clipped the first strand. At once, the rest unraveled around Darcelle's shoulders, flying loose and free.

Darcelle screamed, tossing her magic uncontrolled.

Louisa dodged here to there, avoiding Darcelle's arms sweeping through the air, and cut and cut. Red hair fell in great chunks to the earth.

Soon, only a few pretty wisps of hair remained on Darcelle's head. Her hands flew to her scalp. Around her, all the glittering threads withered and ashed. There were no threads left to obey her, no magic left to call. She staggered backward, as if she did not know how to walk without the weight of her hair on her crown. With her hair short as a pixie's, Darcelle Duval looked no less beautiful, but something within her had dimmed, the glow of magic sucked from her hair and her bones. "No," she whimpered. "It is . . . mine." Her gaze held on the black-and-gold tents beyond the trees.

Louisa drifted toward her. She lowered the shears. "The carnival belongs to no one."

Darcelle's lips curled. She backed away from the gleam of the scissors. Behind her, shadows lined a pathway through the Spark Woods, a twisting road to become lost on.

"You are no longer welcome here, Darcelle." Fiona limped forward, a faint blush in her cheeks that relieved Louisa to no end.

Mercy stood too, her arms slung around Ox's and Jess's shoulders. She glowered at Darcelle.

"Be gone," Ox said.

"Skit-scat," Jess said.

"Good riddance," Mercy said.

Louisa spoke for them all—her friends, of course, and Fiona, Wingless Raven, Lovely Valentine and Bubba Wild, Fire-Red Rosalyn, Mina the Mirror, and of course, her *father*, Quiet Si—when she said, "And never return."

Mercy's shadows nudged and prodded. As soon as Darcelle's foot touched the darkened path, there was no turning back. The carnival closed its borders to her.

Louisa watched her go.

And so, it still held true—no one who was invited to stay at the carnival had ever left it. But Darcelle Duval was no longer welcome, her invitation withdrawn. Though the carnival had once let her in, had loved her and cared for her, it now released her to the Spark Woods, a magicless creature with a heart full of silver barbs, cowering away into the night.

34
MOONLIGHT & MAGIC

Louisa shivered. Only, it was not caused by what lay before her in the forest, but rather what she heard approaching from behind.

Heavy footsteps sounded. So familiar in their uneven tread. Slowly, Louisa turned away from the woods.

Quiet Si strode awkwardly forward, walking so quickly he had to hold a hand to his crinkled, black top hat to keep it from blowing off his head. Beneath it, his hair shone silver, the exact shade as Louisa's tips. Neither of them would ever have the same dark strands her mother had told of in her stories, but still, Louisa and Quiet Si matched in this small way—their hair touched by moonlight and magic.

She held her breath. Tears brimmed in her eyes.

But they were happy tears.

"I saw you." His one pale eye looked from Louisa to the

sky and then back again. She'd soared above the treetops, battling Darcelle Duval, and he'd rushed to help her and all the rest of them. It didn't matter that he'd come late; all that mattered was that he'd come. "You are the daughter of my star."

He sounded uncertain, a tremble to his words, as if he could not quite believe the clouds that had stuffed his mind and sieved his magic were ever so slowly clearing. As if his memories, hazy or long forgotten, might not be irretrievable.

Quiet Si's next step came silently. He floated above the ground the span of one held breath, air beneath his feet and magic in his veins just like Louisa's own, and then he lumbered forward again, his past and present overlapping. It was enough; it was everything. If he could float for one brief moment, one day he again might soar.

"I am *your* daughter," Louisa said, and rushed into his arms.

He folded her close. His embrace was not as soft as her mother's had been (being as he was made, in part, of wood), and he smelled of pine and apples instead of orange blossoms, but she fit into his arms just right. Louisa pressed her face into his black-and-gold-striped jacket. She never wanted to let go.

"I've missed you," she whispered.

Quiet Si placed one hand on the top of her head, as if to make certain she was real and true beside him, not a dream, a figment, a false memory. "I hardly know who I am." His voice sounded ill-used, drowned in apology. "But I know you. I know you now."

"Oh, Father." All the strange bits of him, she already loved. Louisa shook with tears and laughter. She hadn't been sure he would recognize who she was to him. To hear him say it silver-lined the hope she had never let go. "It's really you."

"I did not see the whole of it," Fiona whispered.

But Louisa understood that was the way of misfortunes. The two sides of the coin. What could be foretold and what someone must learn for themselves.

"Ooohhh!" A squeal, and then another pair of arms wrapped around Louisa from behind, squeezing so fiercely she knew it could only be Jess.

And then one after the other, Ox and Mercy and Fiona gathered close, catching Louisa in the biggest hug she had ever been a part of. They leaned against one another, blocking out the cold autumn air and the darkness that lingered. Smooshed right in the middle, Louisa knew she had found a place to call home.

"I knew you'd find him." Ox's voice came close to Louisa's ear. His care and concern wrapped around her before everyone drew apart once again.

"Thank goodness you found *me*." Mercy's voice hushed through the air. "I didn't know if you'd come. If you thought I thieved the magic."

"We know you, Mercy." Louisa used her father's words, which meant so much to her. Nothing was better than being known by someone, than being understood and trusted and loved for being just who you were. "Of course we'd come for you."

"Always," Ox said, as Jess clasped Mercy's hand in her own.

Mercy's eyes gleamed. "Thank you, my friends."

Above them, the sky had darkened to evening. In the distance, music hummed from the carnival. For just one night, it would have to do without their performances. Louisa had so much she needed to say to everyone surrounding her, her father most of all. But the words caught in her throat.

Caught like Darcelle's trapped butterflies. When they'd talked of snaring the butterfly, Louisa hadn't thought she'd be needing to *un*snare any.

But she ran toward the cage of blackened branches, jamming the scissors into the lock until it cracked open, and then she lifted the wooden door and set the butterflies free. They flung themselves from the enclosure, swirling into the air in a cloud of black and gold chaos, and led the way toward the carnival.

"They want us to chase them!" Ox charged ahead, the fastest of them all.

Mercy and Jess, even Fiona, ran after, along the path through the Spark Woods, following the glow of the carnival's lights. Somehow, they seemed brighter, as if the carnival had shoved off the weight of Darcelle's dark shroud. As if it knew she was gone, never to return.

Jess's giggling filled the night.

Louisa took her father's hand, his fingers of bone and wood. Above, the stars twinkled, one more brightly than all the rest. Louisa imagined her mother watching them from the beyond, content at last.

Louisa tightened her hold on her father's hand. He squeezed her fingers. In silent agreement, they sprinted forward, one pair of boots falling heavily, the other floating soundlessly. They wove through the trees toward the carnival, toward the magic.

All the while, Louisa laughed and laughed, her heart full.

But oh, the love bugs were hungry, for they had nothing at all to eat.

ACKNOWLEDGMENTS

I feel like I'm floating thanks to everyone who was there for me writing this book—and for all of you who will be swept up reading this story.

Everyone who touched these pages is made of true magic, especially my agent, Suzie Townsend, and my editor, Brian Geffen. If you two were to join the Carnival Beneath the Stars (and of course, you're invited), you would be gifted your very own names—*Suzie Starlight: Stellar Story Seller* and *Geffen the Great: Tale Tamer.* So many thanks to you both!

I'm also beyond grateful to everyone at New Leaf and Holt/Macmillan, including Dani Segelbaum, Christian Trimmer, Rachel Murray, Jie Yang, Callum Plews, Ilana Worrell, Kelsey Marrujo, Tom Mis, and Madison Furr. Additionally, I am in awe of Katie Klimowicz's amazing book design, Kaja Kajfež's (Iz Ptica) stunning illustrations, and Fiona Hardingham's lovely audio narration.

I never knew how much I needed other writer friends until they magicked themselves into my life. I'm very grateful for Cassie Malmo, Addie Thorley, and Karen Strong. And my G's, Gita Trelease and Gabrielle K. Byrne, I don't know what I would do without you two. Your friendships mean the world to me. Joan He, it's amazing we get anything done for all our chatting and Caly-like loafing—so, so thankful for you, friend.

Hugs and hugs and more hugs for Kara Price, Sara Casiday, and all my lifelong friends, I'm so lucky to know you. For Emma and Molly, my sweet cats, who warmed my lap while I wrote this story, and who I lost last year and miss so much.

So much love to: my mother-in-law, Cynthia Straatsma, you are so bubbly with support and interest in my writing; my grandparents, Esther and Ken Lange, you always ask what I'm working on (and gram, you read even my early drafts); and my pop, Phil Kassner, you probably wish my stories were even weirder.

For my mom and step-dad, Marilyn and Bill Klassy, I am who I am because of you. I love you always and forever.

And for my husband, Cameron Straatsma, you hold my hand and my heart. You mean everything to me. I love you so.